He knew he was in trouble.

Tony was used to guarding middle-aged men in bulletproof limousines, not sylphlike young ladies with violet eyes and cornsilk hair. Maybe he had just been alone too long, but his first sight of Jill Darcy had hit him like a slug to the gut.

Tony parked the car in the paved circle in front of the house and ran up the stone steps. Jill was waiting for him in the front hall, dressed in the same jeans and blue sweater she had been wearing when he left, with a navy pea coat open down the front.

They looked at each other. Tony felt his pulse jump when his gaze met hers.

Yep, he was in trouble.

Dear Reader,

Have you noticed our new look? Starting this month, Intimate Moments has a bigger, more mainstream design—hope you like it! And I hope you like this month's books, too, starting with Maggie Shayne's *The Brands Who Came for Christmas*. This emotional powerhouse of a tale launches Maggie's new miniseries about the Brand sisters, THE OKLAHOMA ALL-GIRL BRANDS. I hope you love it as much as I do.

A YEAR OF LOVING DANGEROUSLY continues with *Hero at Large,* a suspenseful—and passionate—tale set on the mean streets of L.A. Robyn Amos brings a master's touch to the romance of Keshon Gray and Rennie Williams. Doreen Owens Malek returns with a tale of suspense and secrets, *Made for Each Other,* and believe me…these two are! RITA Award winner Marie Ferrarella continues her popular CHILDFINDERS, INC. miniseries with *Hero for Hire,* and in January look for her CHILDFINDERS, INC. single title, *An Uncommon Hero.*

Complete the month with Maggie Price's *Dangerous Liaisons,* told with her signature grittiness and sensuality, and *Dad in Blue* by Shelley Cooper, another of the newer authors we're so proud to publish.

Then rejoin us next month as the excitement continues—right here in Intimate Moments.

Enjoy!

Leslie J. Wainger
Executive Senior Editor

Please address questions and book requests to:
Silhouette Reader Service
U.S.: 3010 Walden Ave., P.O. Box 1325, Buffalo, NY 14269
Canadian: P.O. Box 609, Fort Erie, Ont. L2A 5X3

Made for Each Other

DOREEN OWENS MALEK

Silhouette®

INTIMATE MOMENTS™

Published by Silhouette Books

America's Publisher of Contemporary Romance

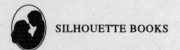

SILHOUETTE BOOKS

ISBN 0-373-27111-5

MADE FOR EACH OTHER

Copyright © 2000 by Doreen Owens Malek

This edition published by arrangement with Harlequin Books S.A.

® and TM are trademarks of Harlequin Books S.A., used under license.
Trademarks indicated with ® are registered in the United States Patent
and Trademark Office, the Canadian Trade Marks Office and in other
countries.

Visit Silhouette at www.eHarlequin.com

Printed in U.S.A.

DOREEN OWENS MALEK

is a former attorney who decided on her current career when she sold her fledgling novel to the first editor who read it. Since then, she has gained recognition for her writing, winning honors from *Romantic Times Magazine* and the coveted Golden Medallion Award from the Romance Writers of America. She has traveled extensively throughout Europe, but it was in her home state of New Jersey that she met and married her college sweetheart. They now live in Pennsylvania.

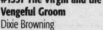

Chapter 1

Jill Darcy was about to acquire a bodyguard.

The notion that she might need one was still difficult to accept. But she saw no way around her father's insistence, which came at the behest of his employers, the federal government, for whom he did chemical research. They were not taking no for an answer, and her father seemed genuinely alarmed for her as well as himself, so Jill was going along with the plan reluctantly.

Jill was up and dressed by six-thirty the day of the newcomer's arrival, but apparently her bodyguard was an early riser, too. When she entered the kitchen at the back of the house he was already seated at the round maple table, drinking coffee with her father. He rose to his feet when she came into the room.

They stared at each other, and Jill acknowledged to herself that even if she wasn't really sure what she had expected, it certainly wasn't this. She assumed what she hoped was a nonchalant expression as she confronted one of the most attractive men she had ever seen in her life. She clenched her fingers into fists at her sides as she tried to maintain her composure.

"Jill, this is Tony Barringer, who will be driving for us," her father said, as if the bodyguard were simply a replacement for Jim, their longtime chauffeur. "Mr. Barringer, my daughter, Jill."

Her bodyguard was about thirty, tall and lean, with wide shoulders and a direct, challenging gaze. He had piercing green eyes, a strong nose and a generous mouth with a full lower lip. Thick, longish dark brown hair loaded with chestnut highlights swept his forehead and touched the collar of the hooded sweatshirt he wore with jeans and running shoes.

"How do you do, Miss Darcy," Barringer said, moving around the table and reaching out to offer his hand.

Jill took it. "I'm fine, thank you," she said evenly.

His hand was large and warm, with a callused palm. His long fingers closed around hers briefly, then relaxed. She felt the current run through her to her toes and was conscious of blushing furiously.

"Your father has been telling me that you're not

exactly happy with this arrangement," Barringer said.

Jill hesitated.

He waited.

"I don't want to seem ungrateful, Mr. Barringer, but a few incidents of childish harassment hardly comprise a crisis, in my opinion. I really wonder if my father and the bureau are overreacting to this situation."

Barringer's expression did not change.

"You disagree?" she asked.

"It's not my job to make that judgment," Barringer replied evenly. "I have been assigned to protect you. It's my job to make sure that no one harms you, and you can be sure that while I am with you, no one will."

Jill stared at him. What exactly was this? Arrogance? Confidence? Honesty?

"I guess I'll have to take your word on that, Mr. Barringer," she replied quietly.

"Tony," Barringer said.

"It's getting late," Arthur interjected, pushing his chair back from the table. "Mr. Barringer has a partner housed on campus who has been assigned to escort me, Jill. I'll be leaving in five minutes."

Jill looked from one man to the other. They seemed to have the situation well in hand.

"Call me Tony," Barringer said, and Arthur nodded. He brushed past the younger man as he left the kitchen.

"Aren't you worried that the bogeyman will get him while he's upstairs?" Jill said, smiling.

"My instructions are to escort you wherever you wish to go," Barringer replied soberly. "That's all."

"And you always follow instructions?"

He looked down at her serenely. "Always."

Jill sighed to herself. This guy seemed just a trifle humor-deprived, like the feds she saw on television dramas, but he certainly didn't look like them. His alluring physical presence was difficult to ignore.

"Even following instructions has its moments," he added in an arch tone.

"I don't doubt it," Jill murmured, glancing away from his green gaze. Despite his youth, he looked like he could tell some war stories.

"I'll try not to interfere with your life too much," he said quietly. "If all goes well you won't even know I'm here."

Jill looked him up and down and then turned away. Did he really suppose that he could become invisible on a college campus where the student body was comprised of sixty percent female students? That would be a neat trick.

She looked back to see him studying her, his eyes narrowed.

"Are you afraid of me?" he murmured.

"No, of course not," Jill replied. In fact, she was a little intimidated by him—he was large and masculine and gorgeous, and had entered her life so suddenly that she was still trying to absorb his presence in it. But she was not going to admit that to him.

"I'm here to help you," he added.

Jill met his gaze but didn't answer.

Her father reappeared, carrying his briefcase and coat.

"Jill, a minute?" her father said, crooking his finger at her.

Barringer went up the staircase as Jill reluctantly followed her father past the living room and dining room on either side of the central hall. They stopped in the spacious, oak-floored foyer, decorated with the Grecian urn planters her mother had brought back from Paris.

"Jill, I want you to do what that young man says," Arthur said sternly.

Jill looked at her father for a long moment and then down at the floor.

"I really don't want a bodyguard, Dad," she began.

"This is no longer open for debate, Jill," her father replied wearily, for they had had this discussion several times. "The man is already here, he's on the job. And I have to say I'm glad. You know how many incidents we've had recently—what if the protests escalate into violence and you become the target? My liaison at the FBI is concerned for your safety, for *our* safety. Once I get to my laboratory, campus security is assigned to watch over me, but you have no protection."

"And I don't need any."

"How can you say that? Just last week a muti-lated doll was found on your desk in the teaching assistants' office!"

"Halloween tricks. If the person who did that was really violent, he or she would not have stopped at a doll."

"That's exactly my point. What will happen next? These people who don't like my research aren't going to give up, and you're right on campus every day, a very convenient target. They have not stopped me by harassing me personally, so maybe now they think that going after my daughter will produce the result they desire. I agree with the FBI. I think you need protection, and I am very happy that the bureau will be providing it for you."

"And I of course have nothing to say about this," Jill observed darkly. She suddenly felt at the point of tears. She had not been wild about the idea of a bodyguard in the first place, and now that she had met the man, the situation was infinitely worse. Since losing Brian, she had avoided any man to whom she felt the slightest pull to eliminate the pos-sibility of more heartbreak. And now she would be forced to spend every day with a man she found desperately attractive. How would she be able to de-fend herself?

"No," her father finally said flatly.

"So I just have to put up with this guy following me around every day?" Jill demanded.

"He will be driving you where you have to go and accompanying you to work, on errands, et cetera. To all outward appearances he will be our new chauffeur.''

"What about Jim?" Jill asked sharply.

"He's sixty-two and ready to retire. The government will be supplying a pension for him."

Well, Jill thought. If the government was willing to supply a pension for their driver in order to put Barringer with her, somebody must really be worried.

"Cooperate," Arthur added. "Tony is here for your protection and you will be protected whether you want to be or not. And you will also keep your opinions to yourself and be civil to him."

Jill shot him a look.

Arthur sighed. "Jill, I know you are shy..."

"I am not shy," Jill said through her teeth.

"All right. You're not shy. But you don't like changes and you're very private, so this situation is tailor-made to bring out the worst in you. Don't let that happen. You can be distant and aloof, and people often mistake that for..."

"A superior, stuck-up attitude?" Jill suggested. Her father's assessment wasn't fair. She couldn't help it if she didn't throw her arms around strangers or know what to say to them.

Arthur considered carefully what to say next. "I know my work and I know you, my dear," he finally said slowly. "Try to be pleasant and have some respect for this man. He is probably no happier to be on this job than you are to have him here. I expect you to behave maturely."

"Oh, all right, I will," Jill said wearily. "I'm not thrilled to have him following me everywhere, but I will cooperate with him."

"Good. Now, I have to go," Arthur said. "Barringer has already put his things in the spare room upstairs. He'll be ready to take you to campus in a few minutes."

Jill reached out to her father before he turned away. "You'll be careful too, Dad, right?"

"Of course. Tony Barringer's partner will keep a close watch on me."

Then he kissed Jill on the cheek perfunctorily and left.

The thought that Barringer would be down for her in a short time made her hands grow cold with nervousness.

Jill went back into the kitchen and put on another pot of coffee. Why couldn't her father go somewhere else to do his research? He insisted that he had already considered that alternative and the facilities at the university were the best, but she resented how his work was dictating the terms and conditions of her life. What her father called "the peace people" were having another rally tomorrow afternoon and Arthur expected there to be some antiwar fallout afterward.

Jill herself found it difficult to be afraid of the peace activists, even though she had been the target of some of their pranks. She felt they had a point. They just wanted her father to stop figuring out new ways to give people anthrax during the next war.

Arthur insisted that his research was not so specific, that the results of his work could be used in many beneficial ways, but the peace group was convinced that his experiments were being conducted for military purposes.

Whatever the truth was, the FBI was interested enough in Darcy's research to supply bodyguards for him and his daughter.

Her mind jumped back to Tony Barringer. She had only seen him for a few minutes, but his impact had been overwhelming. She had never been a believer in instant karma or past lives or the concept of souls bonding at first sight. Until now. She had found him beautiful, but more than that, compelling. When he looked at her with those startling green eyes she could not look away. The thought that he would be living in her house and accompanying her everywhere was tremendously unsettling. His gaze seemed to go right through her, and he loomed over her physically, making her feel small and feminine. And desirable.

Just like Brian. Only with this new man, it was worse.

Jill closed her eyes and heard the ticking of the grandfather clock in the front hall and the hiss of the humidifier her mother had demanded to combat the dry heat in the old colonial. The gathering wind rushed through the eaves and rustled the shutters on the windows. These were the house sounds she had been listening to for many years, but somehow they seemed louder in the wake of the departed masculine voices.

This was just peachy. The fall semester had just begun, and she wasn't two weeks into it before being saddled with a mysterious, sloe-eyed bodyguard who would undoubtedly complicate her life. All because her single-minded father was determined to pursue his research two miles from where they lived in spite of how it affected her. Rather than give it up, he would just bring in some federally supplied "manpower" to protect her.

And in a few short minutes that man had shown himself to be difficult to dismiss.

She stood and pushed her hair behind her ears. No matter how she felt about the bodyguard's arrival, she had a class of undergraduates to teach that day.

She went to collect her books and purse.

Barringer drove the Darcy Lincoln, checking the route he would be taking shortly with the Darcy girl, circling the administration building and then heading for the egress road that connected to the highway. He had memorized the campus map of Eastern Massachusetts University that the bureau had given him. He found it easy to follow the well-marked streets, typical of New England. Barringer had been all over the country and always knew where he was when among the Yankees. They believed in signs.

The leaves on the trees were turning brilliant colors and Barringer should have been able to appreciate their beauty, but he was preoccupied with his first impression of Miss Jill Darcy.

The bookworm he had anticipated had turned out to be a leggy blonde who wasn't delighted to meet him. He wished fervently that he felt the same. His charge was exactly the physical type that attracted him most—tall, pale and willowy. And she was no shrinking violet, either, which he also liked.

Passive women bored him.

He knew he was in trouble.

He was used to guarding middle-aged men in bulletproof limousines, not sylphlike young ladies with violet eyes and cornsilk hair. Maybe he had just been alone too long, but his first sight of Jill Darcy had hit him like a slug to the gut. He had been trained not to show his feelings, but having to hide his reaction to the Darcy girl every day would make this job a whole lot more difficult. He briefly considered asking for a change of assignment, but in eight years of service he had never done so, and the thought of trying to explain why he wanted off the current job made him discard the idea quickly.

It was not the sort of thing the bureau would understand. He had been on the job exactly two hours and exactly nothing had happened. If he tried to convey his problem with this assignment to his boss, the man would put him in for a psych evaluation.

So he was stuck with it. And the necessity of deceiving both the girl and her father about the dual nature of his mission didn't make him feel any better. They knew that it was his job to protect them;

they did not know that Barringer was also in the house to spy on Arthur Darcy.

Barringer glanced at a street sign and turned left. Someone working on a covert weapons project had been passing secrets to a Middle Eastern contact, and Washington knew that the traitor had to be among five people currently employed doing such work. Arthur Darcy was one of the five, and Barringer had been sent to determine if he was the guilty party. Barringer could only imagine how the Darcy daughter would feel about him if she learned about that aspect of his job, but it was his responsibility to make sure she never knew.

As he turned up the hill that led to the Darcy house, he realized that there was a bright spot. Jill Darcy did not know what he was thinking or how he felt. As long as he kept a poker face and did his job, nobody would be the wiser. He was attracted to her, but he wasn't a twelve-year-old with a crush. He would handle it.

The morning sun dappled the foliage and reflected off the windowpanes of the Darcy house as he pulled into the drive. The gracious clapboard colonial, painted white with dark green shutters, sat back in a grove of trees on a bluff overlooking the Connecticut River, which formed the border between Massachusetts and Connecticut. Longmeadow, where the Darcys lived, was the last town in southern Massachusetts before the state line.

Barringer parked the car in the paved circle in front of the house and ran up the stone steps. Jill was waiting for him in the front hall, dressed in the same jeans and blue sweater she had been wearing when he left, with a navy pea coat open down the front.

They looked at each other. Barringer felt his pulse jump when his gaze met hers, but she looked as still and perfect as a Dresden doll.

"You're late, Elliot Ness," she said dryly.

Barringer glanced at his watch. "No, I'm not." He looked up at the grandfather clock. "Your clock is fast."

"Are you the universal timekeeper?"

"I set my watch by the radium clock at Cape Canaveral. It is accurate to a fraction of a second."

"Some people regard compulsive punctuality as a neurotic trait," Jill observed, smiling slightly.

"I doubt that sentiment is shared by the people they must keep waiting."

Jill blinked, amazed. Few people could keep up with her in a game of witty repartee, but this man had no problem. He had an answer for everything, and she was not used to being checkmated at every turn. Brian had been handsome, but not exactly a sparkling conversationalist. So what she had in Tony Barringer was a foil just as alluring to her as Brian had been, but with a nimbler brain and with access to her twenty-four hours a day.

She also was not accustomed to looking up at a man; she was five foot ten and was on an eye-level with most men.

This guy had to be six foot two at least, as he topped her by several inches.

Her fate was clear. She was doomed.

"Well? Are you ready to go?" Barringer asked, interrupting her reverie.

Jill picked up her stack of books.

"I'll carry those for you," he said.

"I can do it."

Barringer sighed and pressed his lips together. "Look, Jill—that's your name, right? Jill?"

"Yes."

"Or do you prefer Miss Darcy?"

Jill shrugged.

"Fine. Whatever. You have made your feelings of reluctance about my presence clear. Nothing you do or say will change the situation. I will be with you every day until my superiors terminate this assignment for me. You can make it tough, or you can make it easy. Either way, I will be here. It's your choice."

"I get the point," Jill said. "End of lecture."

Barringer waited two beats and then said, "Shall we?"

He opened the front door and Jill walked through it, picking up a clean whiff of his soap as she passed him. He followed her down to the car and opened the door on the passenger side, holding it for her.

"Front seat?" she said.

"Do you prefer the back?" he asked.

"I don't care," she said, and slid onto the front seat. Jill met his eyes as he bent to close the door and the shock of the connection went through her once more.

Jill clutched her books to her chest in an unconscious gesture of self-protection as Barringer got in beside her. Who was this guy? Why did she find him so unnerving? It wasn't something she could explain, but she felt it in her pores and under her skin.

"I have to go to the teaching assistants' office first," she announced.

"I know. I'll be coming in with you."

"Will you come to my classes with me?"

"That's right. I already have an auditing pass."

Jill glanced at him quickly. "How did you get that?"

Barringer looked over at her.

"Oh, I get it. Big Brother supplies everything," she said.

Barringer looked back at the road.

"How did you get into this line of work, anyway?" Jill asked curiously. "Did you just show up at the White House one day and announce that you wanted to be a spook?"

A slight tightening of his mouth was Barringer's only indication that he might have resented her question. "Well, you know those hoary old documents, Declaration of Independence, the Constitution, the Bill of Rights?"

"Yes?" She could not help noticing what a fine profile he had, and such long eyelashes.

"Some of us actually believe in them."

Jill looked out the passenger window, stung. She felt put in her place, like a kid who had spoken out of turn. And of course he was right. He had turned her point back on her neatly and made it sound as if she was poking fun at him for having ideals, and that wasn't what she had meant at all.

"Well you do have a strange way of showing it," she finally muttered weakly.

"Why do you say that?"

"Because shadowing me has very little to do with the Constitution. In fact, it could be considered an invasion of my right to privacy."

"Actually, privacy rights can be subordinated for an issue that involves the public good, but you are probably aware of that since you seem to be an expert on the subject," he said.

Jill looked out the window, fuming. He was handling her neatly. She was trying to put him in the wrong, and he would not have it.

"Let's just drop it, okay?" she said tersely.

"Whatever you say, Miss Darcy," Barringer replied mildly, turning onto the highway that led to the main campus drive. They drove in silence until he had entered the south parking lot near the Literature building.

"That sticker entitles you to park in the faculty lot, right?" he added, pointing to the orange-and-black seal affixed to the left side window of the car.

"Doesn't it bother you that your job requires you to pry into the details of your charges' lives?" Jill blurted, disregarding her request to him.

"No, not if it helps me to keep them from harm,"
Barringer replied equably.

"Isn't that a little dramatic? Do you really expect
anybody to 'harm' me?"

"I don't know. But it's not a chance I'm going
to take."

Jill sighed. She was trying to find fault with his
work, and it was clear that he regarded his profession as honorable.

And that he thought she should have the same
opinion.

He got out and walked around the back of the car
to open her door. When she emerged he followed
her into the two-story literature building and up the
steps into the TA office. He identified all of it—the
tiled corridor lined with bulletin boards filled with
fluttering notices, the large TA office with its array
of high-sided cubicles, the library with its double
entrance off to the left—from the floor plans and
pictures he had been given by the bureau.

"Hi, Jill," Michelle Talbot said as she looked up
from her cubicle, then her eyes widened when she
saw the young man following Jill down the aisle to
her desk at the back of the room.

Jill put down her books and said to the man, "I
have some paperwork to do."

"I'll be fine right here," her companion said, taking a seat on a folding chair outside Jill's carrel and
crossing one ankle over the other knee. Jill walked
on to the window overlooking the parking lot. Bar-

ringer looked up and nodded as Michelle passed him.

Michelle waited until she was right beside Jill to whisper in her friend's ear, "You have been holding out on me!"

"What are you talking about?" Jill replied.

"I'm talking about that gorgeous guy with you. Who is he? A new student?"

"Huh. I only wish."

"Then who? Why is he here?"

Jill looked back toward the chair where Barringer was sitting and then led Michelle farther away, to the last window. Michelle was the type who would snoop forever to get the facts if she suspected Jill was not being frank, so Jill decided to tell her the truth. She knew Michelle could be trusted. Jill explained the situation as briefly as possible and then flinched when Michelle squeaked, "You mean he's a fed?"

"Shh, Michelle. Yes, I told you, he's been assigned to drive me, but that's just his cover story. He's really here to be my bodyguard."

"What is he, FBI or Secret Service or something?"

"Or something. My point is, you can't tell anyone. He's my driver and that's all."

"Okay."

"We've been getting a lot of harassment about my dad's work lately from the peace groups on campus. That's why he is here."

"I thought all feds had three-piece suits and buzz cuts."

"Protective coloration, Michelle. He is supposed to blend in on campus."

"Are you kidding? He wouldn't blend in anywhere. Are you telling me you haven't noticed that he is the most attractive man seen walking these corridors since Brian Holdsworth moved to New Hampshire?"

"Oh, please."

"What does that mean? You've gone blind? Your estrogen count is low? Honey, he is hot!"

"He's been assigned to protect me."

"I see. You're upset that he has to follow you around everywhere? I have a great idea, give him right to me. I promise you that I will not complain."

"Be careful what you wish for," Jill said darkly.

"Does that mean we're talking about Brian here?" Michelle asked warily.

Jill shook her head. "Don't make jokes. This guy affects me the same way. It is seriously scaring me."

Michelle looked back at her soberly. "What do you mean? The bodyguard has been with you five minutes!"

"Thirty seconds was enough time. I am constantly in danger of making a fool of myself. I am as attracted to him as I was to Brian, and we know how that ended."

"With him dumping you for Gloria Linklater."

"An experience I am not eager to relive, thank you very much," Jill said tonelessly.

"But this is not the same thing. You're his assignment, this is his job. It's business, right?"

"Tell that to my raging hormones," Jill said, wondering how she would manage to conceal her reaction to Barringer from him as well as everyone else.

Michelle shot Jill an exasperated look and patted the back of her light brown hair. "I know what you need—a distraction. Throw that pile of books into the fireplace and get out of that mausoleum of a house. When was the last time you had a date?"

"When was the last time *you* had one?" Jill countered, grinning widely.

"I mean it. You went out once over the summer with Gil Lyman right after Brian left, and since then nothing, right?"

"Gil Lyman is an idiot. If I can't do better than Gil I'll join a convent."

"You might as well join a convent for as much action as you've been getting lately. What about Jack Greeley? Didn't you see him for a while last year?"

"He's gay, Michelle. I thought you knew that. We were just good friends."

Both women turned as they heard Jill's name called in a masculine voice.

"Somebody up here to see you," Barringer added, watching them come toward him through the line of carrels.

Jill was not pleased to observe that Barringer had been joined by one of her more difficult charges,

Joe Craig. Craig had been in the army and worked for a few years before coming to college, so although he was a freshman he was about twenty-eight. During the two weeks school had been in session he had developed a crush on Jill and was now making a pest of himself.

The wide smile he turned on her as she arrived told her that she was in for more of the same.

"I thought I'd drop by to see if you'd like to meet me for lunch," Joe said to Jill. "The Topsider, my treat."

Jill looked back at him, wondering what it would take to discourage him, and wishing that Barringer were not ringside for this exchange. Craig was about her height and not bad-looking, with a round face and fair hair, but there was just something about him that made Jill want to keep their relationship strictly on the tutor-student level.

"Sorry, Joe," she said briskly. "I'm booked all day."

"How about dinner Friday night then," he said.

"I can't, Joe, I have plans."

"Lunch tomorrow?"

Jill stifled her exasperation and was about to say that her boss did not favor the TAs dating their students when Barringer stood and interjected mildly, "Take a hike, pal. The lady said she's busy."

Craig glared at him. "What business is it of yours?" he said to Barringer, while Jill looked at her bodyguard in outrage and Michelle stared, fascinated.

"It's not my business at all," Barringer replied. "I just get testy when I see some goon hassling a lady and refusing to take no for an answer. So get lost before I lose patience with you."

"You have no right to order me around," Craig said, while Jill closed her eyes, trying to become invisible. The exchange between the two men was acquiring some interested onlookers.

"What difference does that make? I'm bigger than you are," Barringer replied, taking a step closer to Craig.

Craig measured his opponent and opted for a non-combative approach. He threw Barringer a dismissive look and then said to Jill, as if nothing had happened, "You're coming to the advisory tonight at Granny's, as usual?"

"Of course," she replied. Once a week Jill met her undergraduate students for a session at the campus pub. It was a chance for them to air their grievances and ask for advice and academic help.

Craig hadn't missed a session yet.

"See you then," he said, and walked out of the office, not looking at Barringer or the conversation's observers, who were now losing interest and turning away.

"I'll handle my own students, thank you," Jill said frostily to Barringer after Craig left, her expression glacial.

"You weren't handling him very well."

"I didn't need your help!"

"Sure looked like it to me. You wanted to get rid of him, I got rid of him."

"Taking over the management of my students is not in your job description."

"How do I know he's not one of these peaceniks giving your dad a bad time?"

Jill looked at Michelle and then burst out laughing.

"For your information, Mr. Know It All, Joe Craig was in the army for three years, and his favorite topic of conversation is which assault rifle is appropriate for which type of quarry. I doubt he has much in common with the peace activists."

Barringer shrugged. "If I read the situation wrong, I apologize. But I'll be coming along for the pub crawl, just in case."

He walked away from the two women and sat down in the chair he had previously occupied.

"Wow!" Michelle said softly. "Gimme some of that."

"Restrain yourself," Jill said dryly.

"You're not being fair to him, Jill. You did want Craig gone and now he is. Can't you even be grateful? And if you want my opinion…"

"I don't," Jill interjected, then smiled weakly. "All right," she said, throwing up her hands.

"…you should ask Professor Dunleavy to assign Craig to another TA. As long as you are his TA he'll have a convenient excuse to follow you around with his notebook in his hand. I'll take him if you want."

"Maybe I will talk to Dunleavy," Jill said thoughtfully.

"Good."

"Now, I do have a ton of essays to read. Sorry to be so abrupt, but I'm buried."

"Go to it," Michelle said. "I'll see you later."

Michelle went back to her own desk as Jill walked past Barringer to reach hers. Jill glanced back at him as she pulled out her chair. He was watching her impassively, his expression unreadable.

Jill sat and concentrated on her task, trying not to feel the eyes burning into her back.

But she felt them just the same.

Barringer studied Jill's slender form, trying not to notice the waterfall of pale hair that swept nearly to her waist or the long, slender legs tucked neatly under her chair. He groaned inwardly and looked away, sighing.

Why couldn't she have been the four-eyed bookworm he'd been expecting?

The mission had sounded extremely dull, babysitting some academic and his student daughter. Tony knew that he had been given an easy assignment because he had just returned from a tour in the Middle East, but he preferred a challenge and the adrenaline rush of danger. Driving the kid around some sleepy New England town because her daddy was conducting experiments unpopular with a certain segment of the campus loudmouths had sounded like a real snore.

He had entertained himself imagining the daughter while he packed for the assignment in his apartment. According to the notes he'd been given she was a graduate student working on a master's degree in Elizabethan poetry. Her mother had been killed in a car accident when she was ten, she was now twenty-three and had no boyfriend. And from what he had been told, no life. Barringer had pictured a bespectacled grind with mousy hair, sallow skin and ink-stained fingers. The bureau had supplied a clear photo of the father but for some reason the faxed shot of the daughter had been blurred and indistinct, of no use for identification purposes. Tony had chosen not to wait around for another one, so seeing her that morning in her father's kitchen had been something of a shock. He was lucky he had been trained to conceal his reactions because his surprise at her appearance would have been evident otherwise.

Expecting a mudlark, he had shaken hands with Rapunzel.

Barringer shifted his position in the chair and wished for a cigarette. He had quit while undergoing bureau training, but the longing returned at times of stress. By comparison with some of his other assignments the current one should have been a walk in the park, but his attraction to his charge was making him very edgy.

It wasn't a good feeling. He didn't like intangibles like need or desire mucking up the works. He had nothing but a studio apartment, no relatives or pets or plants or debtors, nothing to attend to and no one who would come looking for him in his absence. He traveled light.

Tony Barringer was the only child of a single mother who had died of leukemia during his third year of college. Rootless and with the inglorious prospect of a job in business waiting for him upon graduation, he had been recruited by the FBI through a phys-ed instructor just before commencement. He'd been trained at Quantico in personal protection, and in the past had guarded government officials, ambassadors and visiting dignitaries. This was the first time he had ever been assigned to a private citizen, but he had not expected this mission to be very different from his previous ones. He knew how to keep somebody safe from harm. He'd planned that anyone who came near the Darcy girl would be dispatched quickly, and then hopefully he would have been able to move onto his next, more interesting job.

But that was before he met Jill Darcy, of course.

He couldn't now imagine anyone more interesting to him than the professor's daughter.

Barringer sat up as Jill turned her head and he studied her profile, saw the curving lips, pert nose, sandy eyelashes.

He stirred restlessly and ran his hands through his hair.

He didn't like waiting.

He felt another cigarette pang and knew that was a bad sign. Lately he had been feeling jumpy, suffused with an unnamed restlessness that made him glad of work and keeping busy. Maybe it was just pushing thirty without feeling like he had made any important connection, established any bond that would survive no matter where he went or what happened to him. His work partners changed, his superiors changed, he remained the same. He was a loner, but he had never minded that.

Now, for some reason, he did.

Jill stood up, and he moved to join her until he saw her get a book from a shelf and sit down once more.

Barringer settled back.

Waiting.

It was the worst.

By eight o'clock that night Jill had to admit to herself that Barringer wasn't as much of an intrusion as she had anticipated, although this was not something she would ever say to him. He had accompanied her through her TA session with the undergraduates and three of her master's classes, and aside from interested glances from some of the coeds, he had attracted little attention and seemed to be an expert at making himself unobtrusive. One

professor had inquired about Barringer's presence
and Barringer had flashed his auditing card and an
engaging smile, ending the discussion. During the
Milton class he had seemed interested in the discussion of Satan as the hero of *Paradise Lost,* and during the seminar when the grad students discussed
their individual theses she had been amused to see
him reading a paperback version of *The Prince of
Tides.* She could never forget he was with her,
though; every time she looked over at him he met
her glance immediately with a level, penetrating
gaze that made her turn away quickly.

He was with her, no doubt about it.

Now, as they walked toward the pub and Jill's
meeting with her undergrads, he spoke suddenly and
Jill was startled. He was generally quiet, she had
discovered that day, but still capable of jumping on
you with both feet if you said something he didn't
like.

"What was that?" she said, stopping and facing
him, pulling her jacket closer around her. The autumn evening was cool and fallen leaves swirled
around them and skittered along the paved paths in
the gathering wind.

"I asked if you wanted to get something to eat.
You may not have noticed, but you've been going
all day without a pause for refreshments, and I am
starving."

"Didn't my father give you a hearty breakfast this
morning?" Jill asked sarcastically. "He fancies him-

self quite the short-order cook. I saw dishes in the sink.''

"As a matter of fact, he did not feed me, the dishes were his. And in any event breakfast was fourteen hours ago. Don't you ever get hungry? Thirsty? Tired?''

"Be careful there, buster. Somebody might think you were worried about me,'' Jill said lightly.

"Somebody should be worried about you.''

"Thanks,'' Jill said dully. "I didn't realize it was so obvious that nobody cares.''

"Hey,'' he said, grabbing her arm, alarmed at her reaction. "That's not what I meant.''

"Then why did you say it?'' she countered, and he saw to his amazement that her eyes were filling with tears. Good Lord, could she really be this insecure? How could a young lady so pretty and so accomplished think so little of herself? Is this what happened when a bright, sensitive girl was forced to go through adolescence with a preoccupied father and without a mother's counsel?

"Hey, Jill, come inside,'' Joe Craig called from the doorway of the pub. "We're waiting for you.''

"Let me go,'' Jill said, and yanked her arm from Barringer's grasp. She wiped her eyes quickly with the back of her hand and stalked toward the pub, where the door stood open to the cool night, letting the smoke and beer fumes disperse into the fresh air. Craig stood just inside the door, waiting for her.

Barringer had no choice but to follow Jill into the

loud, smoky interior, crowded with students and anyone else on campus who felt like having a burger or a drink. Jill followed Craig through the crowd to a back table where four other students already sat, waving at Jill when they saw her. Barringer waited until Jill had taken a seat and was involved in a discussion, then he edged his way toward the bar and ordered two sandwiches, a glass of milk and a cup of coffee for himself. He nursed the coffee while he watched Jill and waited for the food. She seemed relaxed and amiable with her students, and he wondered if she only felt comfortable with people when she knew she had the upper hand.

Or maybe she just didn't like being saddled with a stranger every waking minute of every day. He guessed that it might not be his favorite thing, either.

He paid for the grub and carried the paper plates back to Jill's table. She looked up at him narrowly when he placed the sandwich and the cup before her, and he was afraid that she would be stubborn enough to ignore the offering. But after a couple of minutes she began to eat, and when she looked up at him again he smiled at her.

She took another bite.

The meeting lasted a couple of hours, and Barringer was impressed with the way she managed the group, listening to each of her charges in turn and then sharing with the others anything that might help them. By ten the crowd was thinning and Jill's students were peeling off one by one to go home. Craig remained, and Barringer moved forward when Jill stood and Craig stood with her.

"I am going to the ladies' room," Jill announced pointedly, pushing past Craig to the aisle.

Barringer glanced at the back hall, which was labeled Rest Rooms. He followed Jill as Craig said loudly, "Who is that guy? What is he doing here?"

"He's my driver," Jill said quietly.

"Your driver!" Craig snorted. "That's a good one."

Jill kept walking, ignoring the men, and pushed open the door to the ladies' room. The atmosphere inside was thick with the sweet smell of cosmetics and perfume, and the fly-spotted mirror revealed to her a pale face and a harried expression. She pushed into a spot in front of a sink and wiped her eyes with her finger.

She wished Craig would disappear, and she wished Barringer had not caught her off guard with that remark about how alone she was. It was her most vulnerable spot, and she knew she had almost cried when he said it, which had only added to her humiliation. She could just imagine the army of popular, outgoing, bodacious babes who had been hurling themselves on the broad chest of Tony Barringer for years, while she could only attract creeps like Joe Craig and Brian and his predecessors, a long line of suitors who could be summed up with one word: unsuitable.

Jill renewed her lipstick and took a deep, ragged

breath. She couldn't hide in the bathroom forever. It was time to go back out and face the music.

When she walked through the door she went straight into the unwelcome embrace of Joe Craig, who snatched her from the stream of exiting bar patrons and pushed her up against a wall.

"Joe, what are you doing?" she demanded as he pressed his heavy hand across her mouth to silence her, then replaced it quickly with his lips.

Jill struggled, kicking, beating Craig with her free hand while he trapped the other one at her side. She managed to shove him away and turned her head enough to make a sound of protest.

Barringer was leaning against the wall, waiting for Jill, when the sound of a scuffle made him turn his head. He saw Jill struggling desperately with Joe Craig, who had her pinned and was trying, with some success, to kiss her.

Barringer crossed the distance between himself and the wrestling couple in two seconds.

He yanked Craig backward by his jacket collar and flung him against the far wall. He touched Jill on the shoulder and she turned to him, her expression fearful, her eyes wide.

"Did he hurt you?" Barringer demanded.

She shook her head.

Barringer whirled to face Craig, who was staggering back toward him, fists raised.

Barringer caught him with an uppercut and Craig fell back against the wall again, then Barringer kicked his feet out from under him. Craig crashed to the floor and watched from a sitting position, stunned and panting, as Barringer pulled Jill into his arms.

''Play along with me,'' Barringer murmured in Jill's ear, as she registered the strength of his body, which appeared slim but was hard with muscle as it pressed against her. Her face was crushed against his cotton-clad shoulder, and she inhaled his masculine scent through his clothes. She could hear his breathing, harsh from his exertions, and could feel the tension in the arm that bound her to him. She was tucked into the curve of it and his big palm was splayed against her back.

She closed her eyes.

The next thing she knew Barringer had stepped back from her slightly. She looked up at him questioningly and saw his cat eyes narrow, his lips part. Then his mouth came down on hers.

It happened so fast, and was so unexpected, that she had no thought of resisting. She clung to him as his lips caressed hers, the pressure of the kiss increasing as she responded helplessly, opening her mouth slightly as he probed it with his tongue. Her grip on his sweatshirt tightened, then she sighed regretfully as he lifted his head and turned to look at Craig.

''Get the picture?'' he said to Craig. ''Stay away from her unless you want more of the same from me.''

Craig glared at him defiantly but did not reply.

"If there is a next time I'll put you in the hospital," Barringer added. Jill stood flatfooted, in a daze, unable to move.

"Come on," Barringer said to her.

She looked at him dumbly.

He grabbed Jill's hand and hustled her through the pub door as the bartender, who had been watching the fight, rushed to Craig's aid.

As soon as they hit the walkway outside the pub Jill pulled her fingers free of Barringer's and slapped him as hard as she could.

Chapter 2

Barringer flinched slightly. It was his only reaction.

"How dare you take advantage of my predicament that way?" Jill gasped, her face flooding with color. The marks of her fingers turned white on his cheek and his expression was blank, unreadable in the glow of the neon lamps surrounding the pub entrance.

"I didn't see you pulling away from me," he said tightly.

Jill gasped. "You..."

She raised her hand once more and he caught it in midair.

"Don't do that again," he said evenly, holding her fast.

"Why not? You deserve it!"

"I was doing you a favor," he said, releasing her.
"A favor!"

"If that jerk Craig thinks I have a romantic interest in you he will leave you alone."

"And how can you be so sure of that?" Jill demanded, trying to push the too-vivid memory of Barringer's lips caressing hers to the back of her mind. She burned with embarrassment when she thought of her ardent response to him. How could she have been such a fool?

"Because he is afraid of me," Barringer said.

"Oh, really? Then why was he pawing me when he knew you were ten feet away?"

"He was testing me, to see if I would take him on or back down. He didn't like the way our first encounter ended this morning, he wanted to try again, see where he stood. So I jumped him, and left him with the memory of it. He won't bother you anymore."

"Always so sure of yourself, aren't you?" Jill murmured.

Barringer shrugged, then put his hands in his pockets. The gesture made him look very young.

"Bullies always operate the same way. It doesn't take a genius to outmaneuver them," he said, walking away from the pub and indicating that she should follow him.

"So what if he tells everybody? There goes your cover as my driver," Jill said as they headed toward the parking lot.

"He's going to tell everybody what? That I

kicked his butt? Not likely.'' Barringer paused and gazed at her in the silvery autumn moonlight. "Let's assume he does talk. What if your driver were in love with you? Would that be such an awful thing?''

Jill shifted her gaze away from his. "People saw you beating him up," she said stubbornly.

"What people? Aside from you, me and Craig, there was the bartender and that couple so sloshed on beer they would not be able to identify their own mothers in a lineup. By that time everybody else was going home. I don't think we have anything to worry about on that score. But I do want you to get Craig out of your TA section."

"I'll ask for Craig to be transferred," Jill said stiffly. "Maybe Michelle will take him, we have already discussed it.''

"Good. Don't give Craig a reason to interact with you with respect to his schoolwork, and I will take care of the rest.''

"What does that mean? You flatten him if you see him talking to me again?''

"He was doing more than talking tonight.''

"So were you," Jill said.

Barringer glanced at her sharply, then decided to ignore the barb. They had reached the parked car and he unlocked it, opening the passenger door for Jill.

"How did he get to you, anyway?'' Barringer asked. "I saw him heading for the front door when you went to the rest room.''

"The pub put in a new door to the parking lot

just last week, to relieve the crowding at the main entrance. It opens into the hall with the rest rooms.''

Barringer held the door while she got in and then closed it, walking around to the driver's side of the car.

The back door was new, that's why it had not been on the plans of the campus buildings he'd been given. Just a small glitch, but he didn't like it. Tiny bits of misinformation could blow up into big problems.

He had seen it happen.

He got into the car and backed out of the parking spot, gliding onto the campus road. He had driven out to the highway and was halfway to Longmeadow when he realized that the silence in the car was deafening. He looked over at Jill and saw that she was staring at him.

''What?'' he said.

''Drive the girl to her classes, hang out a little more with the albatross, cream the bad guy, all in a day's work?''

''What makes you think you are an albatross?'' Barringer countered softly, not answering her question.

''My father has the impression that this may not exactly be your idea of a dream mission.''

He glanced at her sidelong. ''Oh, I don't know. It's already had its moments,'' he said.

Jill felt herself flushing again. Would he remind her of that kiss every time she got on his nerves? The memory of how she had responded so brazenly to this semi stranger with the hot gaze and the tensile body made her grow warm with shame.

"You told me to play along, so I did," she said.

Barringer gave that statement the reply it richly deserved. He said nothing.

"You kissed me. Don't let it give you any ideas," she added as he pulled into the Darcy driveway.

Barringer stopped the car and turned to face her on the seat. "You're the one who's making a big deal out of it. I seized the situation and I used you to convince Craig that I would break his neck if he bothered you again. That's all. It meant nothing then and it means nothing now. End of story. Is that clear?"

"Perfectly clear," Jill whispered, staring straight ahead.

"Good. Now, let's go inside. Follow behind me so I can check the house first."

He got out and opened her door. She followed him into the dark house and up the front staircase to her room. He opened the door and they went in together. Barringer looked around and checked the windows, the closet, under the bed, then nodded.

"You're fine here. I am going to look around the first floor, make sure everything is secure downstairs. Your father should be asleep, my partner left word that he is secure, but I'll look in on him."

"Okay."

"I'll see you in the morning, Miss Darcy. Good night, sleep well," he said to her.

Jill couldn't look at him. "Good night," she whispered.

She turned away and heard the door close softly behind him. As soon as she was sure she was alone she fell full-length on the bed and buried her face in her arms.

One day with this guy and she had already made a complete ass of herself. She had revealed how his kiss had rattled her and by his own account it meant nothing to him, it was just a means to an end. He would have kissed a life-size mannequin if it would have accomplished the same goal. He had expected her to view his action in the same way he did, as work, and she had shown him just how simple and clueless she was by reacting to it as if it were real. She felt like the victim of a practical joke—unmasked and stupid.

Her experience with Brian had apparently taught her nothing. She had counted on that relationship, opened herself to him, expected it to work out, and had been stunned when he left for a graduate program in New Hampshire, new girlfriend in tow. Well, she would not be left again. It hurt too much to lose people, first her mother to an automobile accident, and then Brian to an ambition he thought would be better served by sharing his life with a woman who had important contacts in his field.

And since she already knew Barringer would be leaving when his assignment was over, she was prepared to invest absolutely nothing in him.

She stood up suddenly and tore off her clothes,

tossing everything onto the floor of her closet and pulling a sleeveless summer nightgown off the shelf. It would do; she didn't have the patience to look for anything heavier. She shrugged into it and pulled the clips out of her hair, letting it down to its full length as she left the closet and tossed the barrettes onto her vanity table.

The room was much as she had furnished it with her mother the summer before Claire Darcy died. Over the years Jill had removed the frilled canopy from the bed and replaced the lace spread, packed up the dolls that used to stand on the shelves and put the board games in the cellar. But the white-and-gilt furniture remained, and the rose-and-ribbon rug, leftovers from her childhood. She was so used to them now that she barely saw them.

It was chilly in her room, but rather than don a robe she chose to light a fire, which the housekeeper left prepared for her on the days she came in to clean twice a week. Jill took a match from the mantel and tried to light the pile of kindling on top of the logs, but nothing happened. She tried twice, three times. She managed to produce only a thin trail of smoke, which died off almost immediately. Disgusted, she threw the match onto the hearth and went to the window, which looked out on the back lawn of the house.

Barringer's room was directly above hers on the third floor, and she could see the pool of yellow cast onto the grass by his light. That room had been empty for years, and seeing the evidence of his occupancy depressed her even further. What was he doing up there, laughing at her? Calling his mysterious superiors on the phone and telling them what a ninny she was?

She turned back to her bed and lay down on it, punching her pillow and staring at the ceiling.

She didn't think she would sleep that night.

Barringer prowled his small bedroom on the third floor restlessly. He had to wait until Jill was asleep to search the house. He took off his sweatshirt and dropped it on the bed.

The Darcy girl. Jill. Not a girl, but a woman. The woman he had kissed when he had no right to do so. He had exploited the confrontation with Craig in order to satisfy his curiosity, but the small taste of the lady's lips had only left him wanting more.

He went to his door and opened it, listening for sounds from below. His bedroom and the room across from it had originally been intended as attic servants' quarters. There was a bathroom in between the rooms that had been modernized to include a stall shower and a new sink. The wind from the river tapped branches from an enormous sugar maple behind the house against the top-floor windows. Out toward the bluff it was dark, and when he went back inside to his window and raised the sash he picked up the dank, tidal smell of the river.

Autumn in New England. From what he'd been told, there was nothing like it.

He was about to find out for himself.

He heard a door slam on the lower floor. Damn it, she was still awake. He leaned against the outer wall of his attic room, closing his eyes.

He could not concentrate on his plan to search the house. He had behaved unprofessionally when he kissed Jill Darcy and then he had lied to her about it. He'd told her that it had meant nothing, that it was just a means to an end, and that wasn't true.

He had used the situation, and her obvious naiveté, to get her into his arms, which he had wanted to do from the first moment he saw her. He had duped her and then made her think that she'd just been a tool used to send a message. He could tell that she wasn't experienced sexually and that his embrace had shaken her, yet he had dismissed it to her, unable to admit to himself that he'd been shaken, too.

He sighed heavily. He didn't feel good about it.

He heard footsteps below and yanked open his door again. He ran lightly down the steps to the second floor before he lost his resolve, then knocked on her door.

"Just a second," she called out. The sliver of light along the floor dimmed for a moment as she moved across the room and pulled open the door.

"What is it, Daddy?" she said as she did so, then her expression changed when she saw her visitor.

"It's me," Barringer said unnecessarily.

She observed him warily. "Yes?"

Barringer tried not stare at her. She was wearing a floor-length sleeveless nightgown of some pale gossamer material that left her slender arms and feet bare. He could see her breasts and trim waist outlined against the gown, backlit by the lamps in the room, and she had released her abundant hair from its confinement. It cascaded over her shoulders and down her back in a champagne flood.

Rapunzel, Rapunzel, let down your hair.

It took all of his willpower not to step into her bedroom and embrace her.

Barringer cleared his throat. "I came to apologize," he said.

"For what?"

"I overstepped my bounds when I kissed you tonight. I shouldn't have done it and I'm sorry. It won't happen again."

She didn't know what to say; his apology was the last thing she would have expected. She saw his eyes drift down to her body again, and when he looked up she felt herself growing warm under his gaze.

"Trying to start a fire?" he said briskly, spotting the thin trail of smoke escaping from the hearth and seizing on the task to get through the awkward moment.

"Uh, yes, not very successfully," Jill replied, looking back at the fireplace.

"Mind if I try?" he asked.

She stepped aside and gestured for him to pass her. He went to the fireplace and knelt before it, playing with a match and kindling until he had a small blaze going. He added sticks to it until it flared up and caught one of the logs. She watched the movement of his back muscles under the T-shirt and the way the firelight made his dark hair shine.

He stood and turned to face her.

"I think it will keep going now," he said.

"I'm impressed," Jill said. "Are you an ex-Boy Scout?"

"Where I grew up the landlord managed the heat in the whole building with a control in his apartment. He kept the place at Arctic level, but the house was built before central heating and each apartment had a fireplace. We learned to use the fireplace."

"Where was that?" Jill asked, as he paused before her.

"What?"

"Where did you grow up?"

"Northern California." He said it in a tone that indicated there would be no further discussion of the subject.

"Thank you," Jill said. She was barefoot and looking up at him. Without shoes she felt even smaller next to his lean height. "For the fire. And the apology."

"You're welcome," he said.

She gazed up at him and felt she couldn't breathe. For a long moment he stared back down at her.

"Good night," he said suddenly, and brushed past her.

"Good night," she called after him, as he went up the steps.

She stood in the doorway looking after him, then turned back into her room and went to bed.

* * *

In the morning Carrie Beckwith, a widow who came in two days a week to clean and leave a dinner for Jill and her father, arrived and made waffles for all three of the house's inhabitants. When Arthur went upstairs to get his coat, Barringer pushed his chair back from the table and said, "Thanks for the great breakfast, Mrs. Beckwith. I really appreciate it."

Both women watched him go into the living room, where the crisp rustle of the newspaper seconds later told them he was reading it while waiting for Jill.

"Polite boy," Carrie commented. "I always was a sucker for nice manners."

"Don't start, Carrie," Jill said darkly.

"What? What am I doing?"

"I am sure my father has already told you everything about Tony Barringer's presence here and my negative reaction to it. Informing me that he's an Emily Post graduate isn't going to make me any more sanguine about it."

"Federal employees are always so correct," Carrie mused, folding a dish towel. "My neighbor's son wanted to go into one of the federal services and the government sent one of their investigators out to ask us about him. A good-looking kid, too, just like this one."

"Humph," Jill said.

She looked at the older woman, who had raised two children on part-time jobs after her husband died early of a heart attack. Jill was very fond of her and admired her tremendously, but if there was anyone nosier than her friend Michelle, it was Carrie.

"He knew I was going to be here today. He greeted me by name when I arrived," Carrie added.

"He was up and dressed when you got here at six?"

Carrie nodded. Jill considered that; the man certainly didn't need much sleep.

"He seems like a good boy to me, Jill."

"He's hardly a boy. I think he's thirty."

"That's a boy when you're my age."

Jill sighed. "Fine. How is Bill doing these days?"

"Don't change the subject. Cooperate and don't give your father any grief about this, you hear me?"

Jill nodded wearily.

"And Bill is just fine. Maureen is pregnant again, did I tell you? It's a girl!"

They discussed Carrie's son and his family until the hall clock chimed, at which point Carrie went into the basement to do the laundry. Jill went into the living room and looked at Barringer, who was dressed in a blue shirt and a leather jacket she had not seen before, and waited several seconds for him to notice her. When he didn't, she cleared her throat.

He looked up from the sports page. "Are you ready to go now? I thought you said ten o'clock."

"There's something else. Something I should have told you before, I guess."

"What's that?"

"I have to go to a mixer Friday night."

He eyed her, waiting.

"It's a social kind of a thing for the students, and the TAs chaperone it and..."

"Mix?" he suggested.

"Yes."

"Are you bringing a date?" he asked neutrally. "Do I have to pick him up?"

"No. No date."

"Okay." He looked back down at the paper.

"That means you have to go, too."

He nodded.

"It's a dress-up thing."

He bit his lip. "Oh, I see. You think I might not have the proper attire?"

"You brought one bag, and judging from its size it could not have contained a suit."

"How do you know that?"

"My father told me."

He folded the paper and put it down on the ottoman next to the chair. "I'll get a suit," he replied.

"How? You make a call and the bureau sends one to the door, by courier? It's nice to have such service."

"I could do that, yes," he replied mildly. "When I'm on a job they send me anything I need for whatever comes up during the course of it. But there's not enough time by Friday. There's a men's clothing store in Longmeadow in the strip mall by the river..."

"Worthington's."

"That's the name. It will be less complicated for everybody if I just fend for myself."

Jill stared at him. Why was he being so nice about this? She had expected him to be annoyed, at the very least.

There were many sides to him, she was learning.

"Want to come with me?" he asked slyly.

She looked at him. She could tell from his bemused expression that he was certain she would turn him down.

"Sure," she said promptly, and was rewarded by a split second of surprise on his face before he stood up and patted his jeans pocket for the car keys.

"Unless, of course, there's some bureau regulation prohibiting the baby-sitter from going on shopping trips with the baby-sittee," Jill amended silkily.

"I have to stay with you so there's not much choice," he replied.

"It's eight forty-five now and Worthington's is ten minutes away. I think we'll have time to get something before I have to get to school."

"What time does the store open?"

"Nine." She paused and gave him the once-over, ostentatiously. "Do you usually need a lot of alterations? They do them at the store, but we only have three days."

"No," he said, looking at her pointedly. "I can usually get something easily."

"Then let's go."

The trip to the store was effortless, since office traffic was over by the time they left the house.

When they pulled into the parking space in front of the just-opened establishment, Barringer looked at the imposing facade and turned to Jill.

"Something tells me they aren't giving anything away here," he said, observing the gold lettering on the sparkling glass windows, the red carpet, the gleaming fixtures, the carved mahogany door.

"Hey, buddy, this was your idea," Jill said, enjoying his discomfiture.

"So it was," Barringer said with a sigh. He got out and opened her door, and together they entered the store.

Three employees converged on them at once, materializing from different points on the large, open floor.

"Would the gentleman require any assistance?" said the first to arrive at Barringer's side, a distinguished-looking man in his fifties with gorgeous white hair and a deferential manner.

"Yes, the gentleman would," Barringer replied briskly. "I need a suit to be ready for Friday."

The clerk, whose name tag identified him as Mr. Faraday, whipped a yellow tape measure out of his pocket expertly as the other two employees retired to their respective corners, as if directed by some hidden signal.

"A forty-two long would be my guess," Faraday said musingly, as Barringer slipped off his jacket and the man went to work measuring his arms, legs, chest and waist. Jill stood by uncomfortably, ex-

amining a stack of shirts across the aisle, not wanting to watch Faraday take his inventory of Barringer's body.

"Excellent," Faraday said. "Forty-two long it is.
I have some handsome selections over here for you
to try," he added, walking toward a rack of the most
expensive suits.

Barringer ignored him, looked around quickly and
selected on another rack of more moderately priced
clothing.

"I'll have three of these—the charcoal gray, the
navy pin-striped and the olive check," Barringer
said flatly, pushing the suits along the rod. "Bring
them to me in the dressing room, please, with a couple of Langwirth shirts and some Bellini ties. Six-
teen thirty-four would be fine for the shirts."

Mr. Faraday made a slight moue of distaste at
Barringer's more modest selections but obeyed,
draping the jackets and unfinished pants over his
arm and leading Barringer to the back of the store.
As the clerk walked toward the dressing room he
gestured to one of the women who had initially approached them to get the accessories.

Barringer disappeared into a curtained cubicle,
and Jill heard his voice asking for different items
periodically, which the store employees handed to
him through the drape. Jill had to admire the way
he handled the obsequious clerks, politely but
firmly. She was always intimidated into buying in-
appropriate things in such situations. Barringer did

not have that problem; he obviously was not fond
of shopping, but he knew exactly what he wanted.

He finally emerged wearing the navy pin-striped
suit with a white shirt and a navy, gray and oxblood
tie. He looked at himself in the three-way mirror
outside the dressing rooms, turning around, and then
glanced at Jill.

"What do you think?" he said.

What did she think? She could hardly tear her
eyes away from him. If he looked great in jeans he
looked fabulous in a suit, even one with the ragged
bottoms puddled around his ankles.

"It looks fine," she said quietly.

"I'll take it," Barringer said to Faraday.

The clerk summoned a tailor, who immediately
began making chalk marks on the suit.

"I'll need this for Friday," Barringer reminded
Faraday.

"It will be ready for you, sir," Faraday replied
politely. "You can pick it up here at the store or we
can send it around to your address, if you like."

"I'll pick it up," Barringer said shortly.

"As you wish," Faraday answered, inclining his
head.

"It'll just take me a minute to get changed," Barringer said to Jill, who nodded.

"You must be so proud, having such a handsome
boyfriend," the female clerk, Mrs. Derry, said
kindly.

"He's not my boyfriend," Jill replied flatly, wondering why she had to say it, since only the two of them had heard her.

"Oh, well, he's a nice-looking friend, then," Mrs. Derry said cautiously, not sure why her remark required such clarification. "He's nearly a perfect size, you don't see that very often."

Jill nodded.

"The only major alterations required are the pants bottoms, that's it," the woman added.

"Yes, that is unusual," said Jill, who had no idea whether it was or not but wanted to end the conversation. She walked away from the woman and toward the changing cubicles, just in time to see Barringer yank the curtain back on his. He was wearing his jeans with the belt through the loops but unbuckled, his top jeans button was open and his shirt was in his hand.

"Uh, I'm sorry. I thought you were with the clerks up at the desk," he said quickly, freezing.

Jill tried not to look at his bare torso, the well-developed muscles in his arms and stomach, the expanse of downy dark hair exposed by the open belt and top button of his jeans. But her gaze was drawn inexorably to his body, lingeringly, and then up to his face.

They stared at each other for a long moment as the silence grew between them. It was broken by Faraday, who appeared suddenly and said politely, "I will need your charge card to complete the transaction, Mr. Barringer."

Jill turned away as Barringer shrugged into his shirt and finished dressing. He gave the card to Faraday and then joined Jill, where she was feigning interest in a stack of leather wallets.

"Ready to go?" he said quietly.

Jill nodded, not meeting his eyes.

He picked up his parcels, got his card back from Faraday, and then they went back to the car.

There was no further conversation about the suit, the dance, or anything else.

"Where is everybody?" Barringer asked as they walked down the deserted corridor of the lit building.

It was the first thing he had said to her since they left Worthington's.

"There's an orientation meeting for the new TAs this morning," Jill said. "I was a TA last year, too, so I was excused from attending it. I already know the ropes."

"You are the only one who was a TA last year?"

"Yes."

"So you were young for the job?"

"I guess so. I took some grad credits over the summer so it gave me a head start."

"So you were like a child genius?" he said, teasing.

"Hardly."

They both stopped short as they rounded a corner and the desk inside Jill's cubicle came into sight.

"Oh, my God," Jill whispered, her hand going to her mouth, her eyes widening.

Her desk was covered with blood, the overflow running onto the tiled floor, and there was a sign propped on a book.

"The Daughter of the Doomsday Doc is drenched in it," the sign read.

Chapter 3

"Stay right where you are," Barringer said sharply. "Don't touch anything."

Jill was happy to obey. She remained at the entrance to the cubicle, trying not to look at the disgusting mess on her desk. She watched as Barringer pulled a tiny Minox camera out of his jeans pocket and began taking pictures.

"Have you had that with you all along?" she asked.

"Tool of the trade," he replied, kneeling and standing and then switching sides, clicking away, hardly pausing to change angles before clicking again. Then she watched, fascinated, as he replaced the camera in his pocket and took out a mini tape recorder and began dictating into it: the date, the time, a description of her desk and its environs as they had found it. When he was finished he said to her, "That isn't human blood, it's from some kind of animal. It's too pale and watery. We have more hemoglobin and collagen in ours."

Jill closed her eyes and put her head back against the wall. The last thing she needed under the present circumstances was a hematology lecture from Mr. Secret Agent Who Knows Everything.

"We'll have to check with biology labs on campus, the animal research facilities, see if any blood is missing."

"We?" Jill asked.

"I'll have to call the local police in on this, although the campus police have initial jurisdiction."

Jill looked at him with eyebrows raised. "Won't that blow your cover?"

"No. The campus police know I am here already. And it's our policy to cooperate with local law enforcement and inform them of any FBI presence in their jurisdiction."

"What are you going to tell them?" Jill asked.

"Whatever they need to know. I got the report on your previous experience, but let's review it—you found a doll on your desk? This desk?"

"Yes."

"What kind of a doll?"

"A kachina, like a voodoo doll, I guess. It had long blond hair and was dressed like me in jeans and a powder blue sweater that I have, except…"

"Except what?"

"There was a death's head on the sweater, on the chest, like an emblem."

He nodded thoughtfully, recalling the details. "And where is that doll now?"

"I gave it to the police, my father insisted."

"And beyond that, I recall harassing phone calls, posters nailed up on campus, picketing your dad's speeches, some unpleasant remarks made to you…"

"Yes."

"So the doll was the first time they came to your workplace and left something."

"Yes, the first time before today."

"And when was your father scheduled to give that lecture on anthrax?"

"Sometime this week, I forget exactly when."

"This—" he gestured to the desk "—could have been a reaction to your father's talk."

Jill nodded.

"It's escalating, even you must see that."

Jill didn't agree with him verbally, but she was privately glad he was with her. The sight of her books and envelopes and her glass paperweight swimming in a lake of blood would remain with her for a very long time.

Barringer looked up as they both heard voices coming toward them, and Barringer gestured for her to step back into the hall. He took chairs from other desks and blocked the entrance to Jill's carrel, making sure nobody disturbed the scene.

"The cops will want to dust for prints. I'm going to call them now." He took a cell phone from his leather jacket and walked away a few feet, talking into it quietly to the local precinct. Jill's fellow TAs arrived from their meeting, slowing up and stopping to stare as they saw the mess on Jill's desk.

"Oh, no, not again," Michelle said, putting her hand on Jill's shoulder. "This is getting scary. Did you call the police?"

"They're on their way."

"Jill, you have to start taking this seriously," Michelle said. "I don't think you can dismiss this anymore. Blood, for heaven's sake. What's next? Your blood?"

Barringer put the cell phone away in his jacket and joined the two women.

"Can't you do anything to stop this?" Michelle hissed in a stage whisper to Barringer. "Isn't that why you're here?"

"Michelle, not now," Jill murmured.

Michelle fell silent and walked away, but she had the look of someone who would have her say in the future.

Two uniformed cops arrived about ten minutes later with the campus police, and Barringer followed them into Jill's cubicle. She saw him show them his credentials and then they took his statement. They looked around and made notes and took a separate statement from Jill. When the local cops were preparing to go, the older one paused next to Jill and said, "This is the second time we've been called out here for this type of vandalism. We're watching this closely, Miss Darcy, and I think you should do the same. Take care of yourself.''

Jill nodded.

The cop glanced at Barringer, and then helped his partner drape yellow tape across the entrance to Jill's carrel.

"Crime scene?" Jill said faintly.

"This sort of thing is a crime, young lady," the cop said. "We have laws that protect private property." He looked from Barringer to Jill. "Any problem with you coming down to the station if we need any further information?"

Barringer said, "No," and Jill shook her head.

"Good." He looked at Barringer and said, "I'll be in touch."

As the policemen left Jill said to Barringer, "I thought the local yokels were supposed to detest the feds."

"Only when the feds behave like the first string and treat the locals like the farm team."

"And I'm sure you avoid doing that," Jill said dryly.

"I find it pays to be respectful," he replied evenly. "It generates cooperation rather than resentment."

"You would rather have them working for you than against you, I guess."

"Something like that." He sighed and ran his hand through his hair. "They are sending a forensics team but I don't think it will do much good. They won't find any prints. Anybody clever enough to get the blood in the first place and then do this when everybody was away from this office would be smart enough to wear gloves.''

Jill shuddered. ''Where do you think the blood came from?'' she asked grimly.

''It was stolen from one of the labs on campus, probably. It's not the sort of thing you can haul around easily, nor is it easy to obtain commercially. You have to fill out forms, answer questions, that sort of thing. The cops took a sample from your desk. We'll know soon what kind of blood it is and that will help pinpoint where it originated. Your father might be of some help there.''

Jill groaned. ''My father. When he hears about this he'll want to chain me in the cellar.''

''He's right to be concerned,'' Barringer said quietly.

''Why? Because we've progressed from voodoo dolls to this sort of thing?''

''Well, yes, partly. Spilled blood is a powerful image. It suggests menace and injury and coming to harm in a violent way...''

Jill held up her hand. ''I get the picture, thanks,'' she said, swallowing.

''And this was focused on you, not your father. Whoever did this is obviously hoping that your father's concern for you will have more of an impact on his behavior than his concern for himself, and cause him to drop his research.''

''That won't happen,'' Jill said flatly. ''They

could leave cadavers with toe tags on my desk and it wouldn't stop him.''

Barringer stared at her intently. "I doubt that very much," he said sharply.

Jill waved her hand dismissively, as if he couldn't possibly understand.

Michelle reappeared and said, "Are you going to cancel your twelve o'clock class?"

Jill shook her head. "No, why I should I? I'm not going to let this hazing interfere with my schedule…" she stopped short.

"What?" Michelle asked.

"My notes for this morning's lecture are in that bloody mess on my desk."

"Want me to check if they are salvageable?" Michelle asked. "Will I get arrested if I cross that tape?"

"I'll do it," Barringer said quickly, not waiting for agreement. He stepped over the tape and into Jill's carrel.

"What, the rules for the rest of us mere mortals don't apply to him?" Michelle sniffed.

Jill looked at her, amused. "I thought you liked him."

"I don't like him in this superfed mode."

"That's what he is, Michelle. He just manages to downplay it most of the time."

"Are the notes you need in a book or something?" Barringer called from inside.

"Blue folder," Jill replied.

He emerged seconds later with the folder in his hand. The edges of it were tinged red.

"I'm afraid it's a bit damp," he said. "The pages are still legible, though."

Jill took it from him gingerly and extracted the handwritten pages from the curling folder.

"This will be fine. The pages are mostly dry and I can read them." She looked into Barringer's eyes. "Thank you."

"No problem," he replied. "I'll explain the missing item to the locals."

"You'd better get moving if you're going to make your class," Michelle said.

Jill looked at Barringer.

"Let's go," he said.

They walked through the lingering crowd, out of the TA office and down the hall to the room where Jill's class would meet.

As it happened they did have to go down to the station house for further questions, and by the time they got home Jill was exhausted and went up to her room to take a bath. She did not reappear for dinner, so Barringer ate the casserole Carrie had left with Arthur Darcy. Barringer spent the two hours reassuring Jill's father that everything possible was being done to apprehend the culprits and that Jill was perfectly safe under his protection.

It was the longest two hours of Barringer's life. He felt sympathy for Arthur, who was concerned enough about his only child to consider abandoning

his life's work. Maybe Jill did not believe Arthur
was serious about this intention, but Barringer did.
But what made it worse was that he knew he was
in the house to spy on Arthur. It was one thing to
search for an unknown, unmet traitor in the abstract,
it was quite another to break bread with a prime
suspect for the treason and come to like him.

Barringer rinsed off the dishes in the sink and left
them in the rack on the drainboard. Jill was still in
her room and Arthur had gone to his study. A long
night stretched ahead of him and he wished he could
use it to search the house. He had to confine his
efforts to the times when both Darcys were sleeping,
and they didn't make it easy with their night wan-
dering and generally erratic nocturnal habits. Neither
one of them kept a regular schedule, staying up late
to work on their projects and meeting with students
at odd hours.

He knew he had his work cut out for him.

He didn't even know what he was looking for,
but he was sure he would know when he found it.
Any evidence of communication with foreign pow-
ers was suspect: letters, phone bills, faxes, shipping
labels. And he had to get into Darcy's computer. He
had come equipped with the password, but he
couldn't exactly stroll into Darcy's office, sit down
at the keyboard and scan the files.

He wasn't even sure where to look. Arthur had a
home office, but there was also a room off the
kitchen that had originally been a porch. It had been
converted into a library and Arthur spent time in

there, too. Barringer also wanted to get into Arthur's lab-office on campus, but that would have to be a midnight venture, possibly with the help of the local police. His partner, assigned to protect Arthur, might have to help.

And on top of all that, he still had to make sure the Darcys were not harmed by the nut jobs pulling these pranks on campus. He planned to call in the report on his cell phone when it was safe to do so, and his colleagues in the home office were not going to be thrilled. It was a pretty strange situation, actually. They wanted him to keep Darcy alive so that he could keep working for them, but at the same time they wanted Barringer to make sure Arthur re- ally *was* working for them, and not against them.

He put water on to boil for instant coffee and sat down at the kitchen table to contemplate his fate. He wasn't happy. With each passing minute he dis- liked his mission more, but he felt trapped into com- pleting it. The job had to be done—if he pulled out they would just send a new person in to finish it.

He didn't want to think about Jill Darcy being guarded by any other man.

She had been a real trooper that morning and he'd felt a surprised admiration for her guts. He had seen people pass out at less grisly sights than a familiar desk covered with blood, but she'd been steady as a rock. She had looked a little green but had gone on with her class as if nothing had happened, refer- ring to her stained notepaper as if it were not pink at the edges and conducting the lecture in a steady

tone. Maybe she had done it out of defiance, a re-
fusal to show weakness to him, but she had done it
just the same. Her behavior today was a pleasing
contrast to the woman who had teared up a short
time ago when she assumed he thought she was
lonely.

There was a real core of strength in her, and he
was glad to discover that.

He had a feeling she was going to need it.

The kettle whistled and he got up to turn off the
gas on the stove. He put the crystals in the cup and
added the boiling water, sitting back down to stir
the hot brew.

He could not stop thinking about the way she had
looked in that transparent nightgown when he went
to her room. The small, perfect breasts outlined
against the material lingered in his mind like something he had seen in a dream. He imagined what it
would be like to cup one of those breasts in his hand,
feel the nipple erect against his palm, then take the
pebble-hard bud in his mouth....

He groaned and crossed his legs. Indulging in sex-
ual fantasies about his charge was the last thing he
should be doing. He must really be losing his grip.
He got up and splashed cold water on his face from
the kitchen tap, drying his skin on his sleeve.

When he turned back to the table, Jill was standing in the doorway to the kitchen, barefoot, wearing
jeans and a loose pullover that was stretched and
faded from wear.

Even in the well-used clothes she looked beautiful to him.

"Hi," she said. "Making yourself at home?"

He smiled. "Having a cup of coffee. Want one?"

She shook her head.

"Feeling any better?"

She shrugged.

"The memory of it will fade. Forensics will be through in your office today, and when you go in tomorrow everything will be the same as it was."

"I really don't think that is possible," she said with a sigh and sat down next to him.

He looked at her intently for several seconds and then said, "What is it?"

"I think I owe you an apology," she said.

"Then we're even," he said. "I owed you one, too, and we made our peace with it. We're quits."

"No, I have to say this. I was not crazy about your coming here and didn't bother to conceal it from you." She paused and looked down at her linked fingers. "When I saw what was on my desk this morning I was very glad you were with me."

Barringer was silent. He knew this was a significant admission; she was ahead of herself academically, but owning up to a mistake was obviously still a big deal for her.

"I just wanted to say I didn't anticipate that the harassment would get this..."

"Ugly?" he said.

She nodded. "I thought the bureau was overreacting to a doll and a bunch of lurid posters."

"And now?"

"Now I'm scared."

"Finally. It took you a little longer than the average bear to realize that they aren't playing."

"It was just inconceivable to me that a peace group could use these terrorizing tactics, and not stop, just get worse. Heckling and nasty signs, yes, but…blood?"

"It's usually that way. They start out with a good cause, but then lose sight of the tactics they're using to reach their goal. Everything gets out of whack and they sometimes wind up being worse than whatever it is they are trying to eradicate."

"Who's 'they'?" Jill asked, smiling slightly.

"Whoever. Crazies come in all forms."

"It can't be wrong to feel passionately about something."

"No, it isn't. And I'm sure that most of the people who are against your father's research are protesting it through the proper channels: writing congressmen, sending letters to the editor, attending legitimate rallies and parade protests with permits, and so forth. But there's a lunatic fringe in most groups and you're feeling the effects of one right now."

Jill nodded.

"My point is, you can *feel* whatever you want. Just don't dump bags of blood on somebody's desk to demonstrate how you feel. If you do that, you're going to attract the unwanted attention of some people in uniforms."

She sighed.

"Speaking of people in uniforms," Jill said, "I talked to Michelle on the phone upstairs and Joseph Allen Craig is now officially a member of her TA group. She can have those stimulating conversations with him about the comparative merits of the AK47, the Uzi and the ever-popular M16."

"Did Craig object to the transfer?"

"No. Michelle said he didn't protest, he seemed happy to move. Maybe he realized what an ass he made of himself at Granny's and is glad to be rid of me."

Barringer was silent. In his experience creeps like Craig did not give up when outmaneuvered by superior forces, they merely changed their tactics.

Jill stood up and lifted her hair off the back of her neck. "I'm going to be burning the midnight oil for a while, so I'll see you in the morning, I guess."

"Okay," Barringer said. So much for his search plans, which would have to wait for another night.

Jill waved and disappeared from the doorway.

Barringer drained his cup and vowed she would never know that he was in her house with an eye to putting Arthur in jail. If all went well Arthur would be exonerated and she would never have to know.

He got up and put his cup in the sink.

If all went well.

The next few days were mercifully eventless. On Friday Barringer picked up his suit on their way back from the campus, and after dinner Jill went up to her room to dress.

She had nothing to wear, of course. She hadn't
bothered to buy anything because she felt she looked
like the Eiffel Tower in everything. She shifted
blouses and skirts around, dismissing each garment
as she touched it, and came upon a dress she had
forgotten. It had been a birthday present from Carrie
a few months ago, and Jill had taken one look at it
and left it in the plastic bag—after thanking Carrie
nicely, of course. It was the sort of dress that required heels, which she never wore, and cleavage,
which she did not have. Still, she studied it, desper-
ate for a change. It was a sophisticated dark sheath
with a V neckline and white piping around the neck,
sleeves and hem. Impulsively she stripped off the
plastic and then took off her clothes, yanking the
dress over her head. She reached behind her neck to
pull up the zipper and then turned to gaze warily
into the mirror.

What she saw there gave her a shock. She
looked…nice. And, was it possible? Sexy! The fitted
bodice elevated and compressed her bust to make it
look more substantial, and the neckline revealed two
snowy mounds set off by the dark material. The
short skirt accentuated her slender legs, and, interested now, she rummaged through the shoe boxes
on the floor of her closet, finally emerging with a
pair of heels she had worn only twice.

She habitually wore flats because she felt that she
towered over everybody, but that would not be the
case with Barringer. She slipped into the pumps and
gazed into the mirror again.

Her pulse began to race. She grabbed an elastic band from her vanity table and twisted her hair on top of her head, something she rarely did—anything that made her look taller was to be avoided. She jabbed bobby pins into the casual knot to hold it in place and surveyed herself again.

She looked great, even she could see that. Her hands cold with excitement, she sat down at the vanity table and redid her hair more carefully, then applied makeup for evening, using mascara and pencil that darkened her fair lashes and brows slightly. She dug out a darker lipstick than the one she customarily used and colored her lips with it. And while doing all this she did not allow herself to consider too closely *why* she was doing it.

She didn't want to look good for Barringer. Of course not.

She just wanted to look good.

That was as far as she was willing to take it. There was nothing wrong in desiring to look nice.

She stood up and got her belted coat from her closet. It looked like the one Ingrid Bergman had worn in *Notorious* and she had bought it on the spot when she found it, even though it had seriously depleted her checking account at the time. She tucked it over her arm and left her room, taking a deep breath as she descended the stairs.

Barringer was waiting for her in the living room. He rose as she entered, giving her one long sweeping glance that went down her body and up again.

''Wow,'' he finally murmured, meeting her eyes.

He was pretty wow himself. He was wearing the suit they had bought and had brushed his normally tumbling hair back from his forehead, which gave him a fresh-scrubbed, "ready for the event" look.

"You look beautiful," he said, and thought that it wasn't a compliment.

It was the truth.

"Thank you," Jill said. "Is my father still here?"

"Campus security picked him up a few minutes ago to take him to his meeting. Then my partner will bring him home."

"So I am your only responsibility tonight?" she asked.

"You got it," he replied softly, reaching out for her coat. As he helped her into it his fingers brushed the back of her neck and she felt the touch run down her spine. He reached ahead of her to open the front door and they went out to the car.

"Is this mixer on campus?" Barringer asked as he helped her into the front seat.

"Yes, in the student union building."

"The student union building?" He looked over at her as he started the car.

"What's so amusing?"

"Nothing. I had almost forgotten about student unions. College seems a long time ago."

"Oh? And what seems current, Father Time?"

"You. And the way you looked when you walked down the stairs tonight."

That silenced Jill until they were parking and she

said suddenly, "People are going to think you're my date."

"I'll make sure to correct that impression immediately," Barringer said dryly. He stopped the car and shut off the ignition.

Jill looked at him. "I don't want you to be uncomfortable," she said.

"I can wear a sign if you like," he went on helpfully. "Driver, Not Date."

"Very funny."

He shrugged. "Just pointing out that there is a solution to your problem." He got out and walked around to open her door.

They marched silently into the red-brick building and followed the sound of band music to the mixer. Crepe paper draped the auditorium, at one end of which was a stage, where the band labored away on "Bridge Over Troubled Water" as couples moved across the waxed floor in three-quarter time. Along the wall a bar had been set up where student bartenders dispensed mixed drinks and beer in plastic cups, and a group of hangers-on lounged in the bar area near a cluster of tables, talking and drinking. Above them a large homemade banner proclaimed "TAs Welcome Grad Students."

"Get me out of here," Michelle said, walking up to Jill as they entered. "Whose idea was this? Except for the booze I feel like I am back in Eastside High School in Chicago." She took a step back and surveyed Jill's dress. "Hey, don't you look smashing. Too bad it's wasted on these yahoos."

"I resent that," Ted Ewing said from behind her. Ted was another TA and Michelle's sometime date. By the look of him he had already had too much to drink.

"Who's your friend?" Michelle asked slyly, looking at Barringer and nudging Jill.

"I'm not her date, but I play one at mixers," Barringer said, running his finger inside his collar.

Michelle giggled and Jill shot her a withering glance.

"I like the suit," Michelle said to Barringer.

"Thanks. Miss Darcy said I could keep it."

Michelle laughed and Jill walked away from him. She heard steps behind her and then Barringer's hand on her arm.

"Don't run away," he said from behind her.

"I feel like running away."

"You do?"

She turned to face him. "You're needling me."

He sighed. "I guess I am."

"Why?".

He stared at her. "Why? Could you make it a little more obvious that you don't want me here? Why don't you get up and make an announcement? I felt more welcome at my cousin Sheila's bridal shower, and Sheila threw me out when she saw me."

She stared back at him. "You're not supposed to feel welcome. You're not supposed to care one way or the other. You're a bodyguard, remember?"

They glared at each other while the band segued

into "Moon River" and Michelle's drunken date danced past them holding a plastic cup of gin aloft like a flag.

"Would you like a drink?" Barringer said to Jill, taking inspiration from the sight.

"What?" Jill said. She had thought they were fighting.

"Would you like to get a drink and sit down? There's a free table over there."

Jill considered the suggestion and then nodded. He took her arm and led her to the open table, where he pulled out a chair and she dropped into it.

"What will you have?"

"Wine, I guess. White or rosé. They're sure to have the best vintage from Minnesota."

Barringer smiled thinly. He gestured to the waiter carrying a tray.

Jill watched the crowd and saw Joe Craig dancing with a girl she did not know.

Barringer got a cup of pink wine for Jill and a dark fizzy brew for himself. He gave Jill the wine and took a sip from his cup.

"What's that?" she asked him.

"Cola. No drinking on the job."

Jill drank and made a face.

"Bad?" he said.

"Not bad if you want to sterilize medical equipment with it." She set the drink aside.

Barringer fiddled with a plastic fork on the table and said, "It was pig's blood, by the way. On your desk."

"You got the report?"

"It came in on my cell phone while you were getting dressed tonight. We're checking all the places where it might have originated on campus first."

"Think you'll find whoever did it?"

"Oh, I'll find him," he said evenly. "Or her, or them. It's only a matter of time."

Jill wondered what kind of childhood had produced such unshakable self-confidence. She had so little herself.

"Your first name is Tony?" she asked.

He nodded, taking another sip of his soda.

"Is that short for Anthony?"

"Antony, actually. No *h*, like Marc Antony. My mother was a history buff."

"And what did your father do?"

"He didn't. He left us when I was two."

"Oh, I'm sorry."

"Don't be. I don't remember him, don't think I missed him when he was gone."

"Did you ever learn what became of him?"

"He went to Australia, can you believe it?" Barringer snorted. "I guess he *really* wanted to get away from us. I never tried to track him. He could be prime minister down there now for all I know."

"And your mother never remarried?"

"No, I gather that the experience with my father was enough to turn her off the idea of marriage for good."

Jill was silent. She was surprised he had revealed so much to her so abruptly.

Barringer asked, "Do you want something to eat? They have some snacks set out over there."

Jill shook her head. It was so obvious that he wanted to change the subject that she felt sorry for him.

"Should you be, uh, mixing?" he asked, glancing around the hall at the crowd.

"It was a triumph of will to get here and show my face. I think I've done my part."

The band, which had taken a break, began to play again.

"Oh, I love this song." Jill sighed as the band launched into a popular ballad.

Barringer regarded her across the table. "Do you want to dance?" he asked.

"Is that permitted, Mr. Barringer? You told me that you always play by the rules."

He didn't answer for a moment, then said quietly, "I don't think dancing is covered in the rule book."

"So it's your call?"

"It's my call," he replied, standing up next to her and extending his hand.

Jill rose also and took his hand. It was warm and dry. He led her onto the dance floor, and as she turned to face him he twirled her expertly into his arms.

Jill instinctively tried to take a step back because she had wound up very close to him; he held her fast, and after a few seconds she realized she did not want to move away. Her senses were engulfed with the size and strength and smell of him; she felt diminished in size as a result, and it was a pleasant change from her usual perception of herself as too tall, too awkward, too something. In his arms she seemed just right. Her face was tucked into the curve of his shoulder and his hand was warm against her back, guiding her across the floor. She had never been led so effortlessly. Jill closed her eyes and let her head rest against his suit jacket, feeling the infinitesimal play of his muscles under the material as he moved easily to the music. Not only was he a wizard at everything else she had seen so far, but he could dance, too.

Jill felt his grip relax slightly and looked up at him. This was a mistake. His face was inches from hers, his eyes at half-mast, shaded by lowering lashes. At close range she saw that his green irises were shot with veins of gold, and that he had nicked the corner of his mouth when shaving that day. His gaze locked with hers and she saw his lips part, felt his breath. He was bending toward her when the music stopped and the couples around them began to clap. Barringer's arms went slack but he did not move away. Jill remained looking up at him until the band jumped into a fast tune and the change startled her, breaking her trance. Barringer said nothing, he just remained looking at her, and it was up to Jill to step back from him.

"I have to talk to Michelle," she said faintly, searching the sidelines frantically for her friend.

Barringer followed her at a slower pace, his expression inscrutable.

Jill spotted Michelle and made eye contact with her.

"Jill!" Michelle called, waving Jill to her side. She was watching the pair coming toward her closely.

"Are you all right?" Michelle said in a whisper when Jill reached her.

"Why do you ask?" Jill said, looking over her shoulder for Barringer, who was standing a few feet behind her.

"Why do I ask? What was that clinch on the dance floor just now? Do you realize what that looked like?"

"He asked me to dance, Michelle. I didn't think it would be a crime to accept."

Michelle stared at her. "Honey, whatever you say."

Both women looked up as Ted staggered past them and then sat down hard on a folding chair, his torso to one side and his legs to the other, his eyes narrowed to slits.

"Oh, Lord," Michelle said. "I have to get him out of here, he is going to pass out cold on the floor."

She went over to him and began to shake his shoulder, and when Barringer saw what she was doing he joined her, both of them trying to get Ted on his feet.

"He's too far gone to walk alone," Barringer was saying as Jill joined them.

"What am I going to do with him?" Michelle wailed. "I can't move him."

"We'll get the car," Barringer said, "and we'll shovel him into it and drive him home. Just wait with him here."

Michelle looked very relieved as Barringer and Jill walked out into the hall. Barringer stopped short and took Jill's arm, moving her behind him, as Joe Craig came toward them from the opposite direction. Craig looked at them, not breaking stride, then looked away as he turned and went into the dance.

Barringer started walking again as Jill tried not to think about how his instinctive, protective gesture had thrilled her.

It's his job, she reminded herself as they got the car and pulled it up to the building entrance. He's being paid to do it.

But it didn't feel that way, and so she was confused.

She followed Barringer inside again and they got Ted on his feet, leaning heavily on Barringer, with the two women supporting him on the other side. They got him to the car and poured him onto the passenger seat, where he collapsed like a folding accordion, sliding onto the floor with his head coming to rest against the glove compartment.

Barringer sat on the curb wearily, bathed in the overhead lighting from the parking lot. "God, this guy is wasted," he said.

"Tell me about it," Michelle replied.

Ted's head fell to the left and he snored loudly, once.

Barringer laughed, and Jill stared at him. She had never seen him laugh. He had very nice teeth, large and white and slightly crooked, the flaws making them look real instead of perfect. His eyes developed crinkles around them when he smiled fully and his laugh was deep and throaty.

Jill didn't want to be more charmed by him than she already was, but it was hopeless.

"What?" he said, sobering as he realized that she was staring at him.

Jill shook her head. What could she say?

"Are you sure that we can get him home?" Michelle inquired anxiously about Ted.

Barringer got up and tried to pull Ted into a sitting position again, but Ted was unresponsive. Barringer's expression changed from amusement to concern and he leaned over the other man, pulling back his eyelids first and then taking his pulse, holding Ted's wrist as he glanced at his own watch.

"What is it?" Michelle said. "What's wrong?"

"He's unresponsive. I don't like it."

"Of course he's unresponsive. He passed out."

Barringer shook his head. "His pulse is slow, looks to me like his breathing is labored, which means his respiratory system is depressed. I think we'd better take him to a hospital."

"Hospital," Michelle moaned.

"Look, your liver can only metabolize so much

liquor at a time. If you ingest more than you can handle you get alcohol intoxication and that can be very serious. Sometimes people left to 'sleep it off' never wake up again. Now, you ladies get in the back and give me directions to the nearest hospital. That's St. Joseph's, right?''

Barringer drove to the hospital and got a staff member there to put Ted on a stretcher and take him inside. While they waited Barringer gave the intake nurse what information they had, and Ted's wallet. Then they sat in plastic chairs done in primary colors until a harried intern with bloodshot eyes came out to talk to them.

''Your friend's blood alcohol level is well above the safe level. You were right to bring him here. We're pumping his stomach to get rid of what he hasn't absorbed yet and then we'll monitor his vital signs until morning. He should be okay but this was a close one.''

Michelle started to cry.

''Can somebody come with me to sign some forms for the insurance company?''

Barringer went with the doctor and Michelle sniffled. ''He's a good man to have around in a crisis.''

''Yes.'' Jill patted Michelle's hand. ''Relax. The doctor said Ted will be okay.''

''I could just kill him,'' Michelle said, wiping her eyes.

''He always drank too much, Michelle. Since we were back in high school.''

Michelle nodded. ''I know. Other people who

went to high school with the two of you have told me.''

''You should tell him to get help.''

''I will, but I don't know if it will do any good. He doesn't listen. I'll have to talk to his parents about it, too, once they get over the shock of this episode.''

Jill glanced over at Barringer and saw him talking chummily with the nurse who had admitted Ted. Their heads were close together and the woman, an attractive blonde, was smiling.

Jill turned her head away and closed her eyes.

A few minutes later Barringer returned and surveyed both women, looking tired, his hands in his pockets.

''Can we go?'' Michelle asked.

''We can. Did Ted pick you up or did you bring your car to the campus?''

''Ted picked me up tonight.''

''Then we'll take you home,'' Barringer said.

Michelle's face crumpled. ''You've been so good to take all of this on, I feel awful about the way this evening turned out for you. I'm sure you never bargained for any of this.''

Barringer lifted Michelle's hand out of her lap and kissed it briefly. ''Think nothing of it,'' he said. ''Now, why don't you two wait here and I'll get the car.''

He said something in a low tone to the security guard by the exit door of the emergency room and then strolled out as both women looked after him.

The security guard moved closer to Jill and Michelle, obviously keeping an eye on them and still in a position to guard the rear exit.

"Oh my God," Michelle whispered. "Jill, what are you going to do about him?"

Jill didn't know what to say.

"Never mind," Michelle said, sighing, when she saw Jill's face. "You've got your troubles, I've got mine. I have to figure out what to say to Ted's parents tonight."

"Are you going to tell them he's in the hospital?"

"I think they'll notice if he doesn't come home, don't you?" Michelle asked miserably.

"I thought he had an apartment."

"He did until recently. He moved back home so he could give up his job and concentrate on school." She dabbed her eyes with her balled up handkerchief. "Of course, the only thing he's been concentrating on lately is the consumption of Jack Daniel's."

Barringer returned and the two women fell silent. He drove Michelle home while Jill relived their dance as she sat next to him. It was impossible to dismiss the feeling of being in his arms; like the kiss at Granny's, the sensation lingered, making her hope for more. Barringer was very quiet as he negotiated the dark streets and only spoke when he had pulled into the Darcy driveway.

"Don't worry about Michelle's boyfriend," he said. "He'll be all right tomorrow."

Jill nodded, not looking at him.

He gazed at her a moment longer, then got out of the car and opened her door.

"It's getting windy," Jill said as she emerged from the car, looking up at the swaying trees. "Fall is here. It will be raining soon, then the snow will come."

"How long have you lived here?" Barringer asked, watching a pile of leaves blow past his feet.

"All my life." She glanced at him as they walked toward the house. "Pretty provincial, huh?"

He shook his head, his strong nose outlined against the dark sky by the porch light. "Roots are a good thing. A sense of home is very important."

"Do you feel that way about any place?" Jill asked as they went inside.

He shrugged. "This country, I guess. The good old U.S. of A. When I'm away I am always glad to get back. The sound of American English is like music to my ears when I return."

"What about your hometown?"

"Oh, we moved around a lot. There's no specific place, unless you consider a series of counties in California a home."

"I've never been out of the country," Jill confessed. "Isn't that ridiculous?"

He stopped and they faced each other in the front hall.

"Not ridiculous," he said. "There's something to be said for knowing your place and thriving there."

"Am I thriving?" Jill asked.

He smiled slightly. "I'd say so."

Jill was drowning in his gaze, sinking and not caring, as if she could breathe under water.

"Thanks for your help with Ted tonight," she said.

"Forget it. Consider it part of the service." He paused, studying her face.

"Walk you up?" he asked.

Jill nodded.

They ascended to the second floor in silence and Jill turned to face him outside her door. She froze as he reached up and removed the pins from her hair one by one, letting it tumble over her shoulders. The silken strands passed through his fingers and she felt the warmth of his touch on her scalp.

"There," he said softly. "The wind started the job, I thought I would finish it."

He held out the handful of pins and she took it.

"Good night," he said.

"Good night," she whispered back.

Jill went into her bedroom and listened as his steps went up to the third floor. She heard his door shut and then shut her own, leaning against it and closing her eyes.

As fast as it had happened, as impossible as it seemed, it was time to face the truth.

She was defenseless against him. She was already looking forward to seeing him every day and dreading his departure. She was as involved with him as she had ever been with Brian, and it had happened so fast she could hardly believe it.

Her heart was at risk again.

Chapter 4

Three weeks passed, during which autumn progressed, the semester labored on, and no further protest incidents occurred. Arthur Darcy was thrilled, thinking that the danger was over, but Barringer remained vigilant, not arguing with the older man but not convinced of Arthur's opinion, either. Darcy wondered aloud why Barringer wasn't taken off the case, but of course Arthur didn't know that Barringer was in his house to spy on him as well as to protect his daughter.

The spying was not going as well as Barringer would have liked, but he hoped that was because there was nothing to find. He searched the house at night as the autumn winds rattled the casements and carried a muddy perfume from the river, prowling the dark rooms with his flashlight and tool kit, alert to any sound of movement that would indicate someone else was abroad. As each day passed he felt guiltier about deceiving the Darcys and more reluctant to leave their house, to go where he would no longer be able to see Jill, and hear her, and occasionally touch her.

That had become very important to him.

He got up now and looked out the window, to see the rising sun through the shedding branches of the tree behind the house. No matter how he felt about Jill, he still had a job to do. The first chance he had he would break into Darcy's computer. It was a last resort, since he didn't think Darcy would store information in such an obvious place, but he had come up with nothing elsewhere. He had been looking for some sort of hidey-hole, some secret book or ledger in a locked drawer; if there was a crime there was always evidence, nobody operated in a vacuum. But he was coming up dry, which meant that the computer was next, and then Darcy's lab at the school, since his partner had also found nothing.

He had no choice about it.

He heard a sound on the lower floor and wondered if Jill was awake. Every night he lay in bed in a sweat, thinking of Jill asleep one floor below him and wishing he could go downstairs and join her. Did she lie in bed and think about him, tossing, tormented by fantasies? Nightly he imagined slipping in between the sheets, gathering her warm and drowsy body in his arms, stripping off the piece of nothing that she wore, stroking her bare and silken skin…

He bit his lip and turned away from the window. Grabbing a shirt from the dresser, he pulled it on over his head and left the bedroom.

He couldn't wait to see Jill.

The autumn rain began that afternoon, and by night the lawns were soaked and the trees swayed and glistened, cascading shining leaves to the pavements. Streets ran with streams that cascaded into sewers and swirled into the puddles that gathered at the bottom of the hill. Jill stood at her window watching the world get wetter, then dropped the curtain and went back to bed. It was 3:00 a.m. by the clock on her nightstand and she had been trying to sleep since midnight.

Jill punched the pillow under her head and then lay staring up at the ceiling, listening to the rain drumming on the roof. Usually she found a rainy night lulling, but this storm was a loud one. In addition, she could not get Tony Barringer, and her feelings for him, out of her mind.

With each passing day she found him more attractive, and she knew if he made a move toward her now she would not be able to resist him. But he remained maddeningly out of reach, quietly doing his job, only hinting now and then at the attraction Jill suspected—and hoped—he felt, but which he kept tightly under control. The memory of his kiss the night Craig had attacked her was never far from her consciousness, but he gave no indication that the experience would be repeated.

A crack of thunder shot her bolt upright in bed. Sighing, she abandoned the prospect of sleep and threw off her quilt. She stood up and felt around for her slippers on the floor in the dark. Maybe a glass of milk would put her to sleep; supposedly there was scientific proof that milk contained a soporific. It was worth a try.

She padded down the stairs and into the kitchen, blinking at the refrigerator light as she pulled out the carton of milk. She poured herself a glass, and as she was replacing the carton she noticed light under the door of her father's study. Arthur was probably working late. Jill got a tray and added another glass of milk and some crackers to it, carrying her burden down the hall and then tapping lightly on Arthur's door with her free hand. She turned the knob and had stepped inside when she stopped abruptly, staring.

Tony Barringer was sitting in her father's chair, operating Arthur's computer handily, screens flashing as he examined files in lightning fashion.

"What are you doing?" Jill demanded, shocked.

Barringer whirled to face her, his face blank. Then he glanced back at the computer, tapping several keys in a row. The information he had been reading shrank from view and the screen went dark.

"How did you get in here?" Jill asked, setting the tray on a side table.

"The door wasn't locked, and I needed to use the

encyclopedia program. I didn't think your father would mind, but I didn't want to wake him up at this hour to ask his permission.''

Jill knew there was a lock on the door, but her father didn't always use it. She also could not tell from the doorway what Barringer had been reading on the desk across the room, but from a quick perusal it hadn't looked like a reference text. She had a feeling he was lying but had no way to pin him down on it.

And there was another troubling consideration. In order to read Arthur's files he would need her father's password, and she had no idea where Barringer would have been able to get it.

"Why did you shut the machine off so abruptly just now?" she asked warily.

"It's storming. Surge protectors sometimes fail, and I didn't want to take a chance."

Or he didn't want Jill to see what he was scouring so intently when she surprised him.

Jill was just about to open her mouth when a streak of lightning illuminated the trees outside the study window with an eerie greenish glow. It was followed immediately by an enormous clap of thunder that shook the house.

Barringer swore and took Jill's arm, guiding her forcefully into the hall.

"Better to stay in the middle of the house, away from the windows," he said, closing the study door behind him.

Jill shook off his hand. "Wait a minute," she said. "Not so fast. I'm not done—"

Barringer put his finger to his lips. "Listen!" he whispered. "Hear that?"

Jill shot him an exasperated glance. He was not going to distract her from getting some answers so easily. Humoring him for the moment, she cocked her head to one side and hissed dramatically, "I hear the rain, that's all."

He shook his head. "Not the rain."

Jill rolled her eyes and was about to offer a sharp retort when they both heard a heavy thud on the front porch.

Barringer looked at her significantly.

Jill shrugged.

Barringer said firmly, "Stay right here. Don't move."

Jill waited until he had gone into the lower hall before following him. She arrived just in time to see him open the front door, his gun in his hand. She had seen it a few times, concealed in an ankle holster, but otherwise had tried not to think about it.

She could see a sheet of rain falling just beyond the portico as the door swung open to the wet dark. Jill peered into it ineffectually, half blinded by the porch light, then gasped as Barringer grunted and jumped back, staggering. An object clattered to the floor as he slumped against the wall, holding his head.

Jill looked down and saw a brick, one corner of it broken and jagged, land against the wall.

Barringer made another sound and Jill flew across the floor to his side. "What is it?" she asked worriedly. "What happened?"

"What are you doing down here?" he mumbled, pushing her behind him with his free hand. "Get back inside."

Jill stared when she saw the blood seeping slowly through his fingers.

"You're hurt!" she gasped. "Let me see!"

"Get back inside, I said," he rasped through gritted teeth. "Do I have to carry you?"

"How did that happen? Is somebody out there?"

"Go!" he barked.

Jill obediently stepped away from the door. "Please let me take a look at that," she said quietly.

He ignored her, inching out onto the porch as she tried to peer past his shoulder. He bent abruptly and retrieved a box from the top step. Jill scampered out of his way as he turned and dropped it on the hall table, yanking the front door closed behind him. He replaced the gun in its holster and straightened up to face her.

"Looks like I interrupted a delivery," Barringer said grimly. "I guess the messenger didn't expect anybody to be awake at this time in the middle of a storm."

The blood from his cut was now running into his eye.

"And so when you opened the door he fired that brick at your head?" Jill said, wincing.

"Something like that." He wiped the flow with his fingers and then glanced at his hand.

"Please let me help you with that," Jill said again. "It looks pretty bad."

He didn't answer, merely turned back to look at the box on the table, then said, "Go into the living room. Wait for me."

"Why? Do you think there's an explosive device in there? Is it ticking? Should we call the bomb squad?"

"It's not a bomb."

"How do you know?"

He looked at her with exaggerated patience. With the gun in his hand and the gore running down his face he resembled the beleaguered hero of an action movie.

"I'm trained to know. But judging from the smell, you won't like it, so let me take care of it."

"I want to see."

He examined her thoughtfully. "Sure?"

Jill nodded.

He took a handkerchief from his back pocket and, using two fingers covered by the cotton, removed the top of the shoe box gingerly. Inside, on a bed of filthy shredded newsprint, was the decomposing body of a field mouse.

Jill turned away, closing her eyes. "Get rid of it, please," she said faintly.

Barringer went into the kitchen and she heard him opening drawers. When he returned a few minutes later he said shortly, "I bagged it. The thing is ev-

idence. There may be fingerprints on the box some-
place or on the note. I also called the local cops to
pick it up.''

''The note?''

He lifted one shoulder. ''More of the same,
threats about your father's research.'' He swiped at
the blood on his face with the crumpled handkerchief in his hand.

After seeing the animal, she did not want to see
the hate mail. ''Please let me take care of your
wound now,'' Jill said, tired of listening to herself
making the same request.

His duty done, he relented. He followed her into
the kitchen and sat docilely as she got the first aid
kit from a shelf. She washed the cut, wincing when
she saw how deep it was and how the blood was
still running freely. His matted hair curled around
her fingers as she tried to staunch the flow.

''I can't handle this, Tony,'' she said, concerned.
''It's too deep. I think it needs stitches.''

He looked up at her when she said his first name.

''I mean it,'' Jill said.

He waved her away, not wanting to hear it.

''I'll drive you to the hospital.''

He reached up and captured her fingers with his,
raising her hand to his mouth.

''No hospital,'' he said, and kissed her palm.

Nonplussed, Jill merely looked at him.

''Thanks,'' he said, and stood.

''Wait a minute,'' Jill said, snapping out of her

daze. "I can't sew you up here in the kitchen, and you are still bleeding like a…"

"Stuck pig?" he supplied, moving past her.

Jill stood in front of him and planted her feet. "For me?" she said gently. "Please?"

He looked down at her. "You're going to drive me to the hospital in your jammies and bunny slippers?"

"Sit back down," Jill said. "I'll change in two minutes." She took ice from the refrigerator and dumped it into a dishtowel, trying not to see the plastic bag of "evidence" on the counter. She put the makeshift ice bag against the wound and took Barringer's hand, placing it firmly on top of the towel.

"Hold that right there," she said. "I'll be back. My father is staying overnight in his lab with your colleague on the job, right?"

Barringer nodded, looking pale.

Jill ran up to her room and tore off her robe, grabbing jeans and a sweater from a drawer. She yanked on the clothes and slipped into loafers, picking up her purse on the run.

When she got back she found Barringer talking to a cop, who left shortly with the evidence Barringer had given him. Blood had soaked through Barringer's towel.

"Are you sure you can drive in this storm?" he greeted her, sounding dubious. "I could ask the patrol cop to wait and take us to the hospital."

"Of course I can drive. Come on. There are two rain slickers in the front hall closet."

He stood up, still holding the sopping towel, and Jill took it from him with one finger and tossed it into the sink. She got a fresh one and handed it to him.

"Just hold that in place, okay? We'll be at the hospital in seven minutes."

Jill had the keys out of her purse and the raincoats in hand as they went through the door. They held the coats over their heads and hustled to the car, which was parked under the portico on the driveway. Jill glanced over at Barringer as she turned the car around and headed for the road. He was sitting back in the passenger seat, the soaking sou'wester over his knees, his head back against the rest, his eyes closed. A trickle of blood ran from his temple down his cheek, mixing with the rainwater on his face. His dark hair was matted to his head in the area of the wound and clinging to the back of his neck in damp strands. His sweater was wet and bloodspattered and the stained towel hung limply from his long fingers like a tattered flag.

He opened one green eye and saw her examining him.

"So what do you think?" he said. "Am I ready for a glossy magazine cover?"

Jill laughed. "Ready for a hospital bed, buddy."

He closed the eye again abruptly. "Don't be so sure about that," he mumbled.

"Just button your lip and rest, okay? We'll be there very soon."

He subsided, and by the time Jill pulled up to the emergency room entrance she was afraid he had passed out while she drove. But when the car stopped his eyes opened. The rain had lessened during the trip, but it was still falling steadily.

"Do you need me to help you?" Jill asked anxiously.

He grabbed the door handle. "No," he said shortly.

He got out on the passenger side and they strode through the automatic doors of the hospital together. Jill followed and watched his progress silently until he was seated in a plastic chair in the waiting room, filling out the forms, a pink-stained gauze square taped to his head.

"Want me to do that?" Jill asked him.

"Doing fine myself," he replied, not looking up at her.

"Who did the bandage? She seemed to know you."

"Triage nurse did it. She remembered me from the time we brought your friend Ted here."

"Why am I not surprised?" Jill muttered under her breath. She recalled the triage nurse—a tall blonde with a wide smile. And she had seemed very interested in Barringer.

"Pardon me?" he said.

"Never mind," Jill replied testily.

He glanced up at her tone. "Something wrong?"

he asked, raising his brows, one of which disappeared into a patch of gory hair.

"Aside from the fact that we are in an emergency room with your head split open in the middle of the night during a monsoon? Not a single thing."

He put the paperwork aside and patted the chair next to him.

"Come here," he said.

Jill eyed him for a few seconds before she obeyed.

"I'm sorry," he said. "You have had a lot to deal with tonight and I'm acting like a complete jerk. I appreciate your bringing me here very much. Thanks."

Now he was making her feel like a spoiled brat who wasn't getting enough attention.

"It's all right," Jill said quietly. "I was just…worried. That's a bad cut."

"They'll sew me up in a few minutes and it will be over, end of story."

"Except for whoever threw the brick."

He held up his hand to silence her as his name was called by the intake clerk.

"Be right back," he said, and spoke to the security guard before he went into the treatment room with a green-garbed medical student.

Jill sighed and sauntered over to a vending machine, plugging in coins to get a can of orange juice. She was swigging from it when she realized that the drumming on the roof had lessened to a faint patter. The rain was stopping.

The guard eyed her warily. What had Barringer said to him?

She selected a ragged magazine from a pile on a table and was trying to read an article on celebrity getaways for the third time when Barringer emerged. He was sporting a new bandage on his head and a shining mop of wet hair.

"Seven stitches," the nurse with him said. "And I washed his hair."

Bully for you, Jill thought as Barringer went to the reception window to finalize his visit.

The nurse disappeared and Jill tossed the juice can into the trash. She watched Barringer pull off his plastic ID bracelet and accept a form from the clerk. He stuck the paper in his jeans pocket and came toward her, smiling slightly.

"All better now," he said. "Let's go."

They walked outside together, into the rain-washed night. Barringer took Jill's hand to help her over a wide puddle and then pulled her in close to his side.

"Relax," he said, hugging her. "It's over."

"No, it's not," Jill said, pulling away from him. "You know it's not. That…thing…in the shoe box was just another form of harassment by the people against my father's work. First signs and catcalls, then animal blood, now dead animals. What's next? And what the heck did you tell the people at the hospital? Did you tell them you were hit by a brick thrown by a nutcase hiding on my front lawn? A nutcase who had just left a mouse corpse on my porch?"

"Not exactly. The nurse was pretty understanding. She cut me some slack."

Jill snorted.

He stopped walking and looked down at her. "What is that supposed to mean?"

"Nothing," Jill said, sighing.

They reached the car and Barringer walked around to open the passenger side door.

"Get in," he said, "I'll drive."

Jill closed her eyes. "You are not going to drive," she said grimly, her fists bunching at her sides. "You have a hole in your head that was just closed with seven stitches and you are full of antibiotics and painkillers."

"I didn't take any painkillers," he said mildly, dragging the toe of his sneaker through a muddy tire track.

"I don't care! You were hurt, you just required medical attention! Can't you stop being a macho fathead long enough to let me drive this car back to the house?"

He folded his arms and surveyed her, leaning back against the rain-spattered car. Mist formed a halo around the streetlight behind his head and a lock of damp dark hair fell over his eyes, making him look careless and boyish.

"You're still spooked, huh?" he said.

"Of course I'm still spooked. Look what happened tonight. Am I supposed to forget that just because some ER nurse patted you on the head and told you to go home?"

"You know, I should be enjoying this," Barringer said, glancing up as a brisk breeze scattered raindrops from a soaking tree branch in his direction.

"Enjoying it?" Jill repeated, staring at him.

"Yeah. When I started this job you told me there was no need for my services and you couldn't wait to send me packing. Now you are so impressed with the seriousness of the situation you want to have a lengthy discussion about it in a flooded parking lot at five-thirty in the morning. I'm amazed."

Jill threw up her hands. "Okay! Do you want me to say it? You were right and I was wrong. I thought, or hoped, that the harassment was over and I was wrong about that, too. Happy now?" She shivered violently and wrapped her arms around her torso.

"I'll be happy when you get in the car and turn on the heat. You can drive." He pulled his sweater over his head and gave it to her. "Put this on now— it's a little stained but it's warm. You're vibrating like a washing machine on the spin cycle."

Jill accepted the sweater, snuggling into it gratefully. She turned on the ignition as Barringer slid into the passenger seat next to her, fiddling with the heat gauge.

"I'm starving," he said. "Is that diner on Canning Street open all the time?"

"You want to go to a diner now?"

"Sure. Why not? We need to talk. Your father is at his lab with my partner but he will be home in a couple of hours. Aren't you hungry? It will be starting to get light soon and last night's dinner seems a long time in the past.''

''Nothing kills your appetite,'' Jill said darkly, backing the car out of the space and heading for the road.

''Got to keep my strength up to deal with you,'' he said mildly, folding his arms.

When she looked at him sharply he grinned at her. The sight of him with the rakish patch showing stark white on his dark head, spikes of damp hair plastered to it, melted her indignation.

Even bandaged like a drunken sailor, he looked good.

''Aren't you tired?'' she asked as the car splashed through a dip in the road filled with water and the windshield was sprayed with scattered muddy droplets.

''Some.''

Jill turned on the wipers and said, ''Doesn't your head hurt?''

''A little, but I've got my second wind.''

''Did they take X rays?''

''I refused them. They wanted to admit me and keep me overnight, but I'm fine.''

''I suppose you also turned down a prescription for pain pills.''

'' 'Say no to drugs,' '' he replied piously.

''What if you need them?''

''Got to keep a clear head to…'' He stopped.

''To deal with me. Yes, I've heard. Can't you take anything else for the pain?''

"They said I could take aspirin." He paused. "Have you got any aspirin?"

"In my purse on the floor," she said.

He retrieved the bottle from her bag and swallowed two capsules dry, putting them into his palm and then firing them into the back of his throat.

Jill coughed just watching him. How could he swallow pills without a drink?

"Did the stitches hurt?" she asked him.

"Nah. They sprayed my scalp with some numbing stuff first and I didn't feel a thing."

"Is your hair shaved under the bandage?"

He nodded. "I'll have a bald patch for a while." He looked at her sidelong. "I am hoping that you'll still consent to be seen with me," he added.

"I'm sure it will only contribute to your rakish charm," she replied dryly.

"So you find me charming, do you?" he teased.

"That's not what I said," Jill answered, and he laughed.

The rest of the short trip was completed in companionable silence. Canning Street seemed to be deserted as they pulled into the diner's parking lot just as the first orange streaks of sunrise were appearing in the eastern sky.

They walked up the concrete steps and entered the railroad car dining room under a pink-and-blue neon sign that flashed "Open 24 Hours."

The booths were already half filled with shift workers having an early breakfast. A hostess with a pencil jammed behind her ear and carrying a stack of plastic-covered menus nodded at them and led them to a booth. She gave them silverware, napkins and water glasses, then deposited two menus and walked away without saying a word.

"Think she's a mute?" Barringer asked, settling into the seat across from Jill and stretching his legs.

"She's probably tired or bored. Hostessing here can't be an easy job."

He picked up the menu and started to read the selections.

"Are we ever going to talk about the subjects we are avoiding? Isn't that why we came here?" Jill said.

Barringer put down his menu and met her gaze directly. "Okay. You go first."

"What were you doing in my father's office using his computer earlier tonight?" she asked.

His breath escaped in a long sigh. "Not beating around the bush, are we?" he countered.

The waitress arrived to take their requests. Barringer waited until she had given them coffee and gone away with their order before saying, "It was exactly as I told you earlier. Your father has a reference CD I wanted to use."

"At three-thirty in the morning?"

"You may have noticed that I don't have a lot of free time, what with escorting you everywhere you go. I decided to use the computer, then when the rain got worse I wanted to shut it off. I apologize for not asking permission first. That's all."

Jill surveyed him as he took a sip of his coffee.

What he said made sense and yet she was uneasy. She kept seeing the look on his face when he turned and saw her standing in the room. He had been very startled, and he had not wanted her there.

"Let's move on to my reason for coming here," he said smoothly. "I know your father had been hoping that the harassment about his research was over, but after tonight we both know that's not true, as you said."

Jill met his gaze but said nothing.

"The local police will want to talk to you when we get back."

"Swell." Jill sighed.

"And my superiors will probably step up security around you as well."

"Step it up? What does that mean? I'll be hand-cuffed to you for the duration?"

"I don't know what steps will be taken. I just wanted to warn you that some changes may be made."

"Why can't the cops find out who is doing this? Why can't *you?* It's not fair for my life to be invaded this way, I didn't do anything wrong!" Jill wailed, then hung her head when she saw a couple of diners turn to look at her.

Barringer placed his large hand over her smaller one. "Take it easy," he said gently.

"I'm sorry. I guess I am getting…scared again. I'm so disappointed. I thought it was over."

"It's not," Barringer said quietly.

"Something about that dead animal… I don't

want to think about the kind of mind that would conceive a plan like that.''

"It's a little more than what was done at the school.''

Jill nodded. "Yes.''

"Well, I'm not glad that you had tonight's experience." He touched the bandage on his head. "Or that I did. But if it has made you take all this seriously again, something good came out of it. An interval with no activity doesn't mean they've stopped. Lulling you into a false sense of security is part of the plan. Just when you think they have given up, they strike again.''

"When do you think they will progress from mice to me?" she asked unhappily.

"Never," Barringer said meaningfully. "Never. I told you that nothing would happen to you while I was on the job, and that still stands. I just want you to be aware that the danger is real and act accordingly, take precautions and listen to me. I promise I will take care of you.''

Jill looked up into his green eyes and believed him.

The waitress arrived with their tray of food and Barringer withdrew his hand.

"Western omelette with toast and home fries, large OJ," she said, putting a plate and a glass in front of Barringer. "And for the lady, English muffin with jelly and cornflakes with milk.''

"Thanks," Barringer said. "And can we have some more coffee, please?''

"Sure thing, kids. Anything for a young couple in love." She winked and marched off to the beverage station.

Silence reigned for about a minute while Jill thought about what it would be like to be in love with Tony, then squelched the idea, angry with herself.

Barringer cleared his throat.

"Sun's coming up," he said brightly, as the waitress returned and poured more coffee.

Jill shredded the muffin, stirred her coffee with a spoon, and tapped the glass that contained the milk intended for her cornflakes. Barringer watched this performance for a while and then said around a mouthful of eggs, "Are you going to eat anything?"

"I told you I wasn't hungry." Jill ripped open her little box of cereal. "I suppose you're more accustomed to voluptuous types who eat like longshoremen."

Barringer paused with a piece of potato impaled on the tines of his fork.

"Voluptuous types?" he said.

"You know what I mean."

Barringer sighed and put down his fork.

"My concern was for your health, not your appearance."

Jill glanced at him warily.

"I am always waiting for you to pass out somewhere."

Jill looked away from him in exasperation.

"But I think you are beautiful."

Jill glanced back at him quickly. He was watching her with a slight smile, his gaze level and measuring. She grew warm under it and observed, "But uppity, stuck-up, reserved."

"I never said that."

"I've been listening to it for years."

"Not from me."

The waitress returned. "Are you guys about done here?" she said briskly.

Barringer nodded. "We'll take the check."

"I'm eating the cereal," Jill informed him, ostentatiously spooning flakes into her mouth as the waitress gave Barringer the bill.

"I'll alert the media." He pulled some money out of his wallet and rose.

"Do you think you'll be able to stop it?" she asked suddenly, reverting to the earlier topic of conversation.

He frowned and brushed his hair back from his brow, his fingers trailing the edge of the bandage he wore. "If I were doing the tracking it would all be over by now. But I'm not. I'm assigned to you. So I have to guard you and just hope that the cops can handle their end of it."

"I'm not impressed with their spectacular results so far," Jill said disgustedly.

Barringer couldn't argue that point, so he didn't. "Finish that up," he said. "I'll be right back."

Jill watched him go up to the cashier and pay the check as she swallowed two more scoops of cereal.

The woman gave him a broad smile as she handed him his change, and Jill looked away.

He seemed to have the same effect on all women. Was she no better than that simpering clerk?

It was not a comfortable thought.

"Ready to go?" he said as he returned.

Jill nodded and got up, following him back outside, where the morning was cool and dry and sunny, the puddles from the storm already evaporating.

They made small talk during the ride back to the Darcy house. They were both spent and it seemed safer to discuss trivia than the real issues that hung unresolved between them. As they walked into the front hall Jill said, "I don't have any classes this morning and I can postpone the TA group. I'm exhausted. I should get to bed before my father returns and wants to have a conversation."

"I'll see if we can do the interview with the police tomorrow."

Jill stepped up to him and raised her hand to his head. "Is it feeling any less painful?" she asked.

"It's fine."

Her eyes filled with tears. "I'm so sorry you were hurt."

"I'm okay now. You took very good care of me."

He bent and kissed her cheek. Jill put her arms around his neck and laid her head on his shoulder. She was so tired and there was no haven she wanted more than the circle of his arms.

Jill felt his lips move in her hair and then touch

her face. She turned her face up blindly for his kiss, and then was startled when his hands came down on her shoulders and he pushed her away gently.

Jill's eyes flew open and she searched his face. He looked back at her briefly, then turned his head so she couldn't read his expression.

"No," he said. "I have a job to do here and kissing you is not part of it."

"You've kissed me before."

"Don't remind me of past mistakes."

"But…"

"Go to sleep," he said brusquely.

Jill practically fled from the hall and ran up the steps to her bedroom. She slammed the door behind her and dove onto the bed, pulling the covers over her head.

How could she so have mistaken Barringer's mood? Hadn't he told her he thought she was beautiful? Hadn't he flushed and looked sheepish when the waitress said they were in love? She was tired of being yanked around by his scruples or his rules or whatever the heck was making him blow hot and cold from one minute to the next.

Jill punched the pillow under her head and resolved to clear her mind of thoughts about Antony Barringer. He was as changeable as a chameleon and she was tired of being buffeted by his whims. She had been acting like an idiot, letting him lead her around by the nose, but that was going to stop.

Now.

He could hook up with that friendly nurse, or go

back to Washington, or go straight to blazes as far as she was concerned.

She closed her eyes and prayed for sleep.

Barringer paced the confines of his bedroom, unable to sit down or stand still. Ever since he had come home he had been restless, his concentration shot to hell. He couldn't think about anything except Jill's stricken face as he pushed her away from him that morning.

He knew he had upset her badly. In addition to finding him in her father's office and then receiving a dead animal in a shoe box, he had rejected her.

Jill had had quite a night.

Barringer was a decisive person; this was one of the few times in his life that he did not know what to do. He had made a mistake in risking the computer search while Jill slept. He knew she was a light sleeper. But since he was with her every time she went out there were not many other opportunities to look at Arthur's files, and time was ticking by with no results on his end. He hoped that he was turning up nothing because Arthur Darcy was innocent, but he couldn't be sure of that until he was satisfied that he had covered the house thoroughly.

And now Jill had caught him in the act, and despite his reassurances, he knew she was suspicious.

She was young and inexperienced and quite a few other things, but she was far from stupid.

Barringer sighed and finally sat down on the edge of the bed, his head in his hands. The first rule of protective training was never to get involved with the subject. And he had not violated it until this assignment. Now he had to choose between hurting Jill and doing his job. He could hardly romance her while trying to nail her father and protect her from whoever was stalking her at the same time.

The situation could hardly be more complicated, and he was so tired of dealing with it he felt like kicking in the walls. Usually he could find an outlet for frustration and turn it into postive energy, but everything on this assignment was new to him. He had no resources to draw from, no background to help him. He was lying to Jill every day while becoming more emotionally involved with her, and he was on the verge of breaking his cardinal rule for himself—that his work did not allow him to have a personal relationship. With anybody, much less the subject of a protective assignment. And he suspected that once Jill learned what he had been up to she would never speak to him again. And finally there was the very real fear that the crazies who hated her father might actually get to her despite his best efforts to foil them. He felt trapped, powerless and stymied. And he saw no way out of the situation. If he asked to be replaced the bureau would demand explanations he did not wish to give and then send someone to take over for him, leaving him crazed with worry about Jill.

It was a mess, and he had no idea how it would end.

Chapter 5

The next day's tension did not foster a lot of conversation. Jill spoke to Barringer only when necessary, and he wasn't exactly chatty, either. They went to the police station in the morning to report on the incident during the storm. Jill answered the questions the police posed and signed her name when requested to do so—she was getting used to the routine. Then she and Barringer went on to the school, still treating each other with deference but never having a personal exchange. By the time they returned to the house in the afternoon Jill was happy to have a respite from his company.

When she was with him, she could not think.

Carrie was putting a pan into the oven as Jill joined her in the kitchen.

"Take that out when the timer goes off and then let it sit covered for ten minutes before you dish it out," Carrie said to Jill, who nodded morosely.

"Why the long face?" Carrie asked.

Jill shrugged.

"Have you been giving that boy a hard time again?" Carrie asked, her eyes narrowing.

Jill stared at her in outrage. "Excuse me. Why is it always my fault?"

"I didn't say that. Let's just say that my opinion is based on long years of experience working in this house," Carrie replied. "I know how you turn in on yourself when you're upset." Her tone softened. "Give him a break, Jill."

"Like I did with Brian?" Jill snorted.

"Brian is one person. Are you going to let him ruin your life, shut you down forever? Tony is a decent guy who deserves to be treated fairly."

"I wouldn't expect you to be impartial," Jill muttered darkly. "Most women don't usually see Tony objectively."

"Where is he, by the way?" Carrie asked.

"Up in his lair, pulling the wings off flies."

"I want him to chop some wood for me. It's warm enough today, but it is supposed to get cold by the end of the week. Your father will want a fire."

"I think that domestic chores are not on his work list," Jill observed.

"He's already agreed to do it, Miss Priss." Carrie picked up the intercom phone and punched a button.

When Barringer answered she reminded him about the task. They both heard him come down the staircase in response and a couple of minutes later the rhythmic sound of chopping began.

"He's so difficult," Carrie said in martyred tones. "I can see what a tough time you must be having."

"He's different with me."

"Yes, I would imagine so." Carrie began to take salad items out of the refrigerator drawer and wash and chop them. She added chives and olives to a bowl and then covered it with plastic wrap. Jill cleared everything away as Carrie made the dressing and put the bottle and the salad bowl in the refrigerator. She washed her hands and then picked up her purse from the table, slinging the strap over her shoulder.

Carrie sighed. "Don't kill each other before I come back on Thursday," she said resignedly, and kissed Jill on the forehead as she passed her.

Jill heard Carrie go out the door and then sat at the kitchen table, listening to the sound of the ax falling in the backyard. Carrie was right, of course. Barringer was not obligated to return her affections. If she had been misled, it was probably her own fault. It wasn't his responsibility if she had been expecting too much and he wasn't prepared to deliver. He had a job to do and she was making it that much harder by throwing herself at him. He was a gentleman and hadn't wanted to be rude, that's why he had seemed to reciprocate. It was about time that she faced the fact that she had exaggerated his response to her, because she had desired so much for it to be real.

In fact, Barringer deserved an apology.

Jill rose from the table and followed the sound of industry to the backyard. What she saw there caused her to pause in the doorway, her breath caught in her throat.

Barringer was chopping logs into kindling, as Carrie had requested. The late afternoon sun was still warm, the porch roof casting a long shadow on the back lawn. His shirt lay discarded on the grass, a neat pile of yard-long sticks to the left of it. He was singing along to the sound of a transistor radio on the picnic bench, imitating James Taylor's falsetto as he cruised through "Handyman."

Jill watched every muscle in his back and arms flex and relax, flex and relax, as he wielded the ax. His torso was streaming with sweat and the hair at his nape was plastered to the back of his neck. His abdominal muscles fanned out from his midline, bunching and rippling as he moved, and a line of dark hair grew down from his navel and disappeared under the damp waistband of his jeans. As he finished each piece he did a little dance step when he added it to the growing pile, then cha-chaed back to position to cut the next one. He was so into the task, so absorbed in the sheer physical pleasure of the work, that he didn't register her presence immediately.

Jill could not tear her eyes away from him. As she watched she felt a tightening in her stomach, a weakness in her knees; she felt her mouth go dry with desire. She had to get away. She wanted him so badly, and she knew that if she faced him now he would know it. He would see it in her eyes.

She was convincing herself to go when he looked up and saw her staring at him as he was walking back to the chopping block. He froze, the ax in his hand, his gaze fixed on hers. Their eyes locked as the tension grew until Jill could feel it pulsing between them, heavy and filled with longing. Finally, he threw down the ax and began walking toward her. When she didn't turn away, helpless to resist, his gait speeded up until he was almost running. When he reached her side he snatched her up in his arms and kissed her in the same movement.

Jill gasped with shock as his mouth found hers, then she surrendered, all thoughts of her planned apology flying from her mind. If she had caught him at a weak moment, then so be it. She was unwilling to deny herself one moment longer for his principles, his career or her own lingering doubts. She might suffer loss again, as she had with her mother, as she had with Brian, but nothing was more important to her than responding to this man in this moment.

She would take Tony for as long as she could have him.

Barringer kissed her repeatedly, sinking his fingers into her hair, bunching it in his fists. Jill reciprocated his passion, running her hands up his bare back, slick with perspiration from his work, clinging to him, caressing the muscles that contracted at her touch. His skin was hot from his exertions and redolent of sun, sweat and the soap he had used that morning. The combination was an aphrodisiac to her; she opened her lips and felt his probing tongue, the smooth surface of his teeth. She drew her hands across his wide shoulders, up the cords in the back of his neck and into the damp curls at his nape. She had been kissed many times by various boyfriends, come close to making love with one of them, but something about Barringer's embrace was different from what she had previously experienced. He wasn't tentative, or searching, or even coaxing—he knew what he wanted and seemed certain she wanted it, too. But of course in addition to her behavior the night of the storm, he had seen the way she'd just been looking at him.

That could hardly have left him in any doubt.

Barringer lifted his mouth from hers and picked her up, kicking a toolbox out of the way as he carried her up the backstairs and onto the converted porch. He set her down on the wicker divan and fell full length with her, twining his jeans-clad legs with hers and rolling her under him. His kisses fell randomly on her throat and down into the neckline of her blouse as his fingers roamed through her hair, running the long, pale strands over his palms. When his mouth moved lower and stopped at her breast she gasped and held his head against her, watching his eyes close luxuriously as he mouthed her through her shirt, his black eyelashes a stark contrast

with the flushed skin of his face. She lay pliant as
he lifted his head slightly to unbutton her blouse, his
eyes slitted and fixed on her body. When her breasts
were revealed he made a slight sound deep in his
throat and sought them with his mouth again. He
put his tongue into the cleft between them and then
brushed his lips across the scrap of lace that covered
one pouting nipple. He pulled the bra cup back as
he drew her to him, and his mouth closed hungrily
over her breast. Jill groaned aloud and locked her
legs around his hips as he sucked the rigid peak,
reducing her to a reciprocal bundle of nerve endings,
her entire being focused on the sensations he was
evoking.

He shifted slightly and pulled her bra and blouse
off with one motion, burying his face between her
breasts, his superheated skin scalding her, his beard
stubble abrading her. The pain was pleasure. He
locked his hands behind her waist and teased her
mercilessly, laving her with his tongue, his soft hair
and soft mouth against her skin driving her to clutch
him closer, rocking her hips against his. He grunted
and pressed her down, hard and full against her
thighs as his mouth returned to hers and he whispered against her lips.

"I have wanted this for so long," he muttered,
sounding as drugged as he looked as she gazed up
at him. His thick dark hair, a mess from her caresses,
fell over his forehead and his lips, swollen and wet
from her kisses, showed red against the whiteness
of his teeth. His eyes were hazy, his lids half low-

ered, his voice low and intimate. "I have stayed awake so many nights and thought of you like this, in my arms, in my bed…." The sentence trailed off as he kissed her again, running his palm down her side and lifting her skirt, smoothing the length of her leg with his hand. Jill sighed and threw her head back as he caressed her.

"Jill, where are you?" Carrie's voice called from inside the house.

Barringer sprang to his feet, pulling Jill up with him and yanking her blouse into place. He grabbed her discarded bra and stuffed it into his pants pocket, adjusting his jeans in the process.

"Button your shirt and go talk to her," he said breathlessly in a low tone. "I'll be outside."

He dove headlong through the back door just as Carrie came into the kitchen.

"I'm out here," Jill called, trying to button her blouse with fumbling fingers, dazed from Barringer's lovemaking and sure the lingering effects of it would show on her face.

"What are you doing on the porch?" Carrie asked as she appeared in the doorway, a grocery bag in her arms.

"What are you doing back here?" Jill countered, pushing her hair back from her face. "I thought you had left for the day."

"Your father had asked me to pick up a few things and I remembered it on the way home. So I just did the shopping and came back. Why didn't you take the casserole out when the timer went off? Your dinner is ruined.''

''I fell asleep on the divan, I'm sorry,'' Jill lied. ''I guess I didn't hear it. Don't worry, we'll order a pizza. It's not like we haven't done it before.''

''Are you okay?'' Carrie asked, peering at her.

''Sure, why not?''

''I don't know, you seem…strange. Flushed or something. Have you got a fever?''

''No, of course not. I'm fine.''

''Then why did you fall asleep?''

''I don't know, I haven't been sleeping very well at night. Really, Carrie, don't worry about me.''

''Your blouse is buttoned wrong,'' Carrie observed.

Jill looked down at herself, cursing mentally. She rebuttoned rapidly, wishing that Carrie were not quite so sharp. Why did she have to see so much, ask so many questions?

''And what happened to your underwear?'' Carrie added, as Jill strode forward and took the bag out of the older woman's arms.

''I was changing when you came in,'' Jill answered. ''Give me that and go home. You've done enough for today.''

Carrie had the look of a woman who was not quite satisfied with what she was hearing, but she nodded. ''Okay. Where's Barringer?''

''Still outside, I guess.''

Carrie glanced out the back window. ''Looks like

he cut plenty of wood. He should be finishing, it will be dark in an hour. Make sure you feed him.''

Jill nodded, wondering how long she could keep up this calm facade without screaming.

''Okay then, I'm off,'' Carrie said, waving goodbye. Jill listened to the sounds of her departure for a second time, hoping that she would stay gone.

About a minute after Carrie's exit Barringer appeared, coming through the door with Jill's bra in his hand.

''I saw Carrie's car pull out of the driveway,'' he said.

From his guilty expression Jill could tell what else he was going to say.

''Save it,'' she said, snatching her garment from his hand and throwing it on a chair. ''I don't want to hear any speeches or sermons now, not after your wrestling match with me on this couch not ten minutes ago.''

She sat on top of her bra and burst into tears.

''Did it feel like I was wrestling with you?'' Barringer asked quietly, sitting opposite her.

''You know exactly how it felt. Forget it. Carrie came just in time. Go upstairs and brood or scribble in your diary or plot my destruction or whatever the heck it is you do up there.'' Jill wiped her streaming eyes with her fingers and sniffled loudly.

''I should never have let it get so far today,'' he said. ''It's all my fault.''

''Damn right it is,'' Jill responded, starting to cry again. ''It's your fault for moving in here and taking care of me and making me feel the way I do and then playing hard to get when I...when I..." She broke down again and started to sob, hating herself for the loss of control but unable to keep it together.

He made a move toward her and put his hand on her arm. She shrugged him off.

"Don't worry," she said, gasping. "I will make no further attempts to ravish you. And since my looking at you in a certain way seems to create a physical response from you that we certainly would not want to happen again, I will try not to *see* you in future. How's that?"

He got up and took her by the shoulders and shook her, hard. "Stop it," he said grimly. "Stop it right now."

Jill fell silent, staring at him. She had never heard this tone from him before; he was furious.

He released her and walked away from her, pacing the narrow confines of the booklined porch. He was still shirtless and she tried not to stare at his naked back, his tan from the previous summer just fading, the ridge of his spinal column showing slightly under the taut skin. Her gaze caressed the lean muscles of his arms as he turned to face her. He had a white scar from an old injury on his left bicep and a small brown birthmark just above his collarbone.

"Do you think this has been easy for me?" he demanded tightly. "Being with you every day and yet being forbidden to touch you? Having to smell your scent, your fragrant shampooed hair, your skin after you have bathed and perfumed it? Your legs in skirts, your breasts in a tight sweater and your hips in jeans, your ankles, your wrists, your mouth. Every part of you drives me crazy. I am parched for the taste of you, starved for the feel of you, so hungry to have you that I can't sleep at night. I wouldn't wish my state of mind for the last month on my worst enemy, and that's the truth."

Jill was silent, astonished. This was the longest speech he had ever made, and its content thrilled her and yet frightened her at the same time. He sounded as if there were no way out of his dilemma.

"Can't you just ask to be reassigned?" she said feebly, after a protracted silence.

He laughed derisively, which was not the reaction she had expected. "Do you really think I care about my job at this point?" he demanded incredulously. "You just don't get it, do you? If I quit or ask for a transfer they will send somebody else and I will be forbidden to see you at all. Working for the bureau is not like working for the local discount chain. You don't turn in your resignation and just walk away. The terms of separation are unique in each case, and I have seen enough departures to be sure that mine would include no further contact with the subject family, namely you and your dad. I would be perceived as a failure, and failures aren't rewarded with season tickets to the people they have not been able to protect. And the worst is I would be replaced by somebody else who may or may not be competent, and I would be left to wonder whether the nut jobs who are after your father had gotten to you in some way I could only imagine in my most gruesome fantasies.''

He stopped to take a breath, and Jill wondered at his sudden candor. These were certainly the most revealing words he had said to her since she met him.

''Tony, tell them anything. What does it really matter what you say?''

He was staring at her. ''God, you are so naive. I sometimes forget how young you are.''

''I am six years younger than you are, Methuselah.''

''But you have no experience of the world, Jill. There's a lot more at stake here than you know. There are things about this case that I can't tell you....''

''Why not?''

''Just take my word for it. I can't get involved with you as long as I am on this job, and I have to stay on this job until whoever is harassing you is caught and put away permanently.''

''Get involved? How delicately you put it.''

''What do you want me to say? Do you prefer that I use more graphic terms?''

''I would prefer that you tell me the truth!'' Jill shot back, and then the phone rang.

They started as if they had been interrupted by a gong.

''Let it go, don't answer it,'' Barringer said tersely. ''Let the machine pick it up.''

"It may be my father," Jill said, ignoring him and walking into the kitchen.

"Hello?" she said into the receiver, still looking at Barringer, who had followed her.

As soon as she heard the voice on the other end Jill knew she had made a mistake by insisting on answering the phone. She listened for a moment and then closed her eyes.

"Perfect," she said, holding the phone up to indicate it was for Barringer.

"Who is it?"

"Your girlfriend from the emergency room, Nurse Nancy," Jill replied, covering the earpiece with her hand. "Or Judy I think she said her name is. Judy Campbell. She sounds all aflutter, don't keep her waiting." Jill jammed the telephone receiver into his midsection and stalked past him into the hall and up the stairs. She went into her room and locked the door.

She had been sitting on the bed for less than two minutes when Barringer began knocking.

"Go away," she said mulishly.

"If you don't let me come in and explain I will kick the door down," Barringer answered grimly, in a tone that indicated that he meant what he said.

Jill got up and unlocked the door.

"You don't have to be such a Neanderthal about it," she muttered, not meeting his eyes.

"Oh, really? Would you have opened the door meekly and invited me in like a good little girl if I hadn't?"

"Good little girls don't invite bossy, overbearing, secretive, know-it-all Neanderthals into their bedrooms," she replied darkly. "And I'd like to see you explain the broken door to my father."

"You let me worry about your father," Barringer said crisply. "Now, are you going to listen to me?"

"I'm listening," Jill said grudgingly. "Not that you owe me any explanation, of course."

Barringer sat opposite her on the edge of the bed and replied quietly, "I owe you an explanation."

She turned away from him, not answering.

He put his forefinger under her chin and gently moved her face back to him.

"Look at me," he said.

She raised her eyes to his.

His green gaze was guileless and direct.

"You remember the first night I met Judy, when we brought Michelle's boyfriend to the ER?"

Jill nodded.

"Judy told me that people as young as Ted who drink to the point of unconsciousness are most likely alcoholics. They aren't usually identified as such until they are older, when their drinking habits start to cause real problems. College-age drinking tends to be dismissed as just kids unwinding and having a good time. Anyway, the other night when I was at the hospital again we talked about a rehab clinic that a friend of her uncle's runs near Boston. The friend is a doctor who specializes in the treatment of alcoholism in young people. I asked her to get the name and number of it from her uncle to give to

Michelle. Judy called me back today to give me the information.''

"And to keep in contact with you."

He smiled slightly. "She could not possibly have had selfless motives?"

"Not in your case. And I'm sure Big Brother would have no objection to your hitting the sheets with her, right? Just what you need—a little relaxation with no career obstacles to muddy up the works.''

"Jealous?" he said softly.

Jill's eyes filled again.

"She's after you," she said miserably.

"She's not going to get me."

"Hah!" Jill said, but her lower lip was trembling. "I saw her sashaying past you in that sexy uniform.''

Barringer bit this lip to keep from laughing. "What? That fetching polyester smock with the full-length apron and the sensible rubber-soled shoes?"

A single tear slipped onto Jill's lower lashes and caught there, trembling. "You can't tell me you didn't notice that she was playing up to you."

"I didn't notice," he said, smoothing her hair back from her brow and wiping the tear away. "I haven't been able to see any woman but you since I met you."

Jill watched him come closer and then closed her eyes slowly as his mouth found hers. He put his arms around her shoulders and pulled her down to the bed with him, turning her toward him and embracing her fully. He kissed her repeatedly, deep, drowning kisses that left her breathless, yet eager for more. Then he dragged his parted lips over her throat and down to her breasts, covered now by just a thin layer of silk. Jill dug her nails into his shoulders, gasping when he tore at the buttons and then threw the blouse on the floor. The sensation of his bare skin against hers when he embraced her again was a renewed shock and she stiffened slightly. He ran his hand down her spine, relaxing her, and she fell back in his arms to allow him access to what he most wanted: her body, which he had craved but had been forbidden to touch.

He made a soft growling sound as he sucked and nipped and laved her, then lifted her off the bed, pulling her across his knees and sweeping her skirt to one side. His hand skimmed up her leg as he continued to kiss her half-naked body, caressing her ankle, her knee, then pushing her waistband back to tongue her navel and sliding his fingers under the band of her panties. She groaned and thrust helplessly into his touch, far too excited to resist him or think of anything but the bliss of this submission in his arms. She wrapped her arms around his neck and licked the scar on his bicep, his collarbone, his flat nipple encircled with dark hair. He released the button on her skirt and eased the zipper down its track, finally lowering her, clad only in her pants, to the bed. He drank in the sight of her, his cat eyes roaming her body hungrily, and he was bending to resume making love to her when the telephone rang shrilly. Again.

"I am going to rip that jack out of the wall," he said through gritted teeth, looking over at Jill's nightstand, where the telephone stood. Then his expression changed and he released her. He sat up suddenly, his head in his hands.

"I am an idiot," he said fiercely. He stood up and looked around wildly as the telephone continued to ring.

"What? What is it?" Jill demanded, her pulse still racing as her heart sank.

"The time! I was supposed to report in by phone to my superior fifteen minutes ago. Don't answer the phone, I'll call in and take care of it. Where is my shirt?"

"On the back lawn, last I saw it," Jill replied, pulling the bedspread around her shoulders as Barringer ran through her bedroom door and into the hall. She heard him pounding down the stairs and realized that he hadn't even said goodbye to her.

The job meant more to him than she ever could, no matter what he said.

Just like Brian, who had dropped her for a grad student with connections in his major and an open slot at an Ivy League university.

She fell back on the bed, drained, her body still burning from Barringer's touch, her lips still wet with his kisses.

Damn him. She just couldn't muster up another ounce of indignation or outrage. After two furious lovemaking sessions in one day with a man who wanted to run away from her as much as he wanted her, she was too exhausted.

She would make sure that he would never leave her in this position again.

Barringer returned half an hour later and he joined Jill and her father eating the pizza Jill had ordered with the salad Carrie had made. Barringer waited until Arthur had disappeared into his study and then said to Jill as she was unloading the dishwasher, "We have to talk."

Jill didn't even turn around to look at him. "There's nothing to say. I thought about everything after you left and you're right. It would be a mistake for us to get involved. There's just too much against it. We're two mature adults and we should be able to get through this without falling into bed together. It's just a case of proximity, anyway. We're both young and healthy and we've been thrown together for protracted periods of time. It was inevitable. But in the real world we would not have five minutes for each other and I think we should remember that."

There was a profound silence behind her as she stacked dishes on the counter. She finally turned around to face him and saw that he was staring at her, a blank expression on his face.

"What's the matter?" she asked innocently. "I'm agreeing with you. Is the prospect of that so amazing it has left you mute?"

Barringer pressed his lips together and eyed her speculatively. He didn't say, "What fresh hell is this?" but she knew full well that he was thinking it.

"I have a lot of papers to correct, so I'll go to my room," she added quietly.

"Just a minute," he said as she tried to brush past him. He put his hand on her arm and she stepped away from him.

Even the slighest touch was dangerous and threatened to set off another brushfire.

"You're supposed to go to Boston on Friday for that conference. I'll have to go with you."

"What's the problem? That we might have to stay in a hotel or something if it runs late? Don't worry, I promise not to take advantage of you. I'm too noble a person to compromise your virtue."

"Can't you get someone else to go in your place, or postpone your appearance?" he asked, ignoring her sarcasm.

"No, I can't. This has been planned for six months and I won't disappoint the people who asked me to come. They'll be left with a hole in their program and nobody to fill it. I will show up there and give my talk as planned."

He eyed her intently, then looked away.

"Now, may I go upstairs and get to work or do you want to discuss something else?"

He pursed his lips and Jill could see him reining in his temper with an effort.

"We'll leave at ten on Friday. Your speech is at one so that should give us plenty of time."

"Fine."

Jill stalked up the steps and Barringer heard her door slam on the second floor. He grabbed the kitchen trash can with the pizza box sticking out of it and lugged it down to the garage, seeking relief in physical activity so he wouldn't start breaking things.

He didn't blame her, not really, as much as her flip replies stung him. From her point of view he was toying with her, and when his assignment was over he would disappear. She thought he was amusing himself with her until he could go back to his old life, after which she would never hear from him again.

She simply did not understand that despite his best intentions he couldn't keep his hands off her. His double lapse today was proof of that. But if he wanted to keep her safe, as well as find out if her father was a traitor, he had to do just that.

He dumped the contents of the can into the trash barrel and jammed on the lid.

He had to do it.

Carrie came and went on Thursday, tiptoeing around the house as if she were walking through a minefield, and Jill went about her routine as if Barringer were invisible, which was fine with him. The less said the better. They had both talked too much, and revealed too much, already. By the time they got into the car for the drive up to Boston on Friday they had reached a wordless level of detente. This only disguised the turbulent feelings that lay beneath the surface of their civility, but it was enough that they could get through the trip without veering into personal issues. For the moment, they had to be satisfied with that.

The morning was chilly and gray and it was easy to see that winter was closing its cold fingers around the northeast; the warm day earlier in the week would be the last one.

Barringer was a competent driver. He consulted a road map several times, stopped once for take-out coffee and got them to the outer Boston suburbs before a light powdering of confectioner's sugar started to fall past Jill's window.

''Hey, what's that?'' he asked, peering through the windshield. ''I checked the weather report three times and I swear that snow was never mentioned.''

''Welcome to New England,'' Jill said dryly. ''Anyway, it won't stick, it's too wet. It will melt on the roads.''

''Thank you, captain of the ski patrol. Isn't that what the Donner party said before they started out for the pass? You must know that snow changes with a temperature drop. Like the temperature drop that nightfall usually brings?''

Jill was silent. He was right, of course, but she wasn't going to give him the satisfaction of telling him so.

He hunched over the map to find the right highway exit, and once they were on the city streets Jill pointed the way to the college where the literature conference was being held. They parked in the student lot when she showed her guest pass to the guard, and Barringer gave her his parka as they got out of the car.

"Take it," he said, when she protested. "You'll be soaked by the time we get inside and you have to give a lecture. I have a down jacket and some other stuff in the trunk for later, but I don't want to delay now. Come on."

Jill gave in and donned the heavy jacket, which came to her knees and hung over her wrists. They searched the venerable campus for the right stone building, and when they found it went inside immediately to get warm. Barringer took her coat, then took off his sweatshirt and shook it free of snow. He hung both garments on a rack above an ancient radiator that hissed steam into the tiled hallway. He got them cups of coffee from an urn at a welcome station and then they went in search of Jill's assigned room, where Barringer settled in the audience to listen to Jill's talk.

The chairs filled up and a monitor distributed programs. Barringer saw Jill's name on the list and realized that she was lecturing undergrads on her subject of choice, which was "The Love Poetry of Andrew Marvell." As she broke down the verses of "To His Coy Mistress," he smiled as he applied them to his own life and then his smile faded as he looked out a side window and saw that the snow was now steady and driving, a full-fledged storm.

Jill had barely left the podium to the sound of applause before he sidestepped her and ushered her into the hall.

"It's coming down heavily, we have to go right now," he said. "There are only a couple of hours of daylight left."

While Jill went back into the reception area to say goodbye, Barringer filled his thermos with coffee from the reception table at the back of the room. He was hoping they would not have to stop on the way home.

He didn't want to waste any time.

Jill was talking to another woman when he appeared, threading his way through the crowd to her. He nodded and smiled at Jill's introduction to her companion, not even listening to her, and then pulled her by the hand toward the door.

She shrugged him off as they reached the front steps of the building. Then she stopped short when she saw the slanting drive of the snow and the small, dry flakes.

"Right," Barringer said as the severity of the situation registered on her face. "Let's go."

She followed him to the car and then sat quietly as he backed it out onto the road and then headed for the first intersection, slowing to a crawl as he approached the light so he wouldn't skid across the road. He retraced his arrival route to get back to the highway, but everything looked different in the fading light, and when Jill directed him to a shortcut to the main road she had used the last time he was in Boston, he took it. The shortcut led them out into the country. By the time he realized there was no crossing road to take them in the right direction it was nearing dusk and he was on a one-lane cattle track through open fields.

He slowed the car as he looked around him, trying to get his bearings.

"Are we stopping?" Jill asked.

"No, we're not stopping," he answered, obviously preoccupied.

"You don't know where we are?"

"I don't know where we are," he confirmed.

"We've gone about four miles since we took this road," Jill advised him.

The car idled as he snapped on the overhead light and unfolded the map. After a brief study of it he said, "I think we took the wrong shortcut, Jill."

Jill looked properly chagrined. "I shouldn't have suggested that, I'm sorry. I thought it would save us some time. I guess I was thinking of another road."

He glanced over at her and smiled.

"Hey, don't worry about it," he said. "You were trying to help. The thing to do is turn around and go back to where we took this turn. Then we should be able to get back on the right track."

Jill looked away, unable to reply. At a time when she already felt bad and he had every right to make her feel worse, he was comforting her. He might have taken advantage of a weak spot where her libido was concerned, but his basic decency was unassailable.

He started moving again. The car trudged along through the deepening snow as Jill watched him drive and a tense silence filled the car. As he turned the wheel to go back the way they had come the left rear tire slipped into a ditch by the side of the road. The car lurched to a stop. Barringer threw it into reverse but the wheels just spun uselessly as the motor whined.

"What is it?" Jill asked worriedly. "What happened?"

Barringer put his arms across the top of the wheel and rested his forehead on his crossed hands.

"Well, if I had to guess, I'd say we're stranded."

Chapter 6

"Stranded? How can we be stranded? Can't we push the car out of here?"

"No, we can't. The car is on an angle, can't you feel it? It's just not a matter of pushing it forward, you'd have to push it up and out of the trench, and this thing weighs a couple of tons. We need a tow truck." He reached into his pack on the back seat and pulled out his cell phone, flipping its switch with his thumb. He watched the tiny screen light up and then said resignedly, "No signal, it's just roaming. I was afraid of that."

"What are we going to do?" Jill asked evenly, trying not to sound alarmed. It was almost dark and they seemed to be in the middle of nowhere.

He looked past her out the passenger side window

and said, "There is a building across that field, a barn or storage shed of some sort. We'll head for that."

"Can't we just stay here and run the heater?" she asked, not wanting to leave the warm haven of the car.

"I am not sure, but I would bet money the tailpipe is blocked with snow," he said. "If we just stay here the exhaust will back up into the car and kill us. Plus even if I could get under the car and free the tailpipe I don't know how much fuel would be required to keep the heater on all night. If we ran out of gas we might freeze to death. The temperature is thirty degrees now but the sun is just setting. I don't know how much more it will drop overnight."

Jill turned and looked at the dim outline of the barn in the distance. "How far away do you think that is?" she asked.

"A mile and a half, maybe two? It's difficult to judge over this flat distance, but we can walk it. The good news is that there's a chimney on the side of it, which means there is a fireplace or stove inside. If there is anything made of wood in there we'll burn it to keep warm tonight. But we'd better get cracking because it will only get colder as we sit here talking."

"I am dressed all wrong for hiking through snow," Jill said miserably. "I'm sorry."

He held up one finger, turned off the motor and went around to the back of the car. She knelt on the front seat and watched anxiously as he slid partially

into the ditch in order to reach the trunk, and then
emerged from its depths with a coat in one hand and
a pair of boots in the other. Her rubber boots. He
slammed the trunk closed and climbed back onto the
road, picking his way over the slippery terrain and
coming to the passenger door. He had her father's
battery-operated lantern draped over his arm.

"I took this stuff out of the front closet at your
house," he said, handing her the rubber boots and
a pair of waterproof mittens and a knit hat from the
coat pocket. Then he donned his down coat and
zipped it up smartly, setting the torch at his feet.

"You brought all this stuff just in case?" she
asked, amazed, peering at him through the curtain
of falling snow.

"'Semper paratus,'" he said. "'Always prepared'. The FBI motto. Or maybe it is the Boy
Scouts, I forget." He shouldered his backpack resolutely.

"I will never make fun of J. Edgar Hoover
again," Jill said fervently as Barringer reached into
the car and shut off the ignition, then clicked all the
locks down with the master button. He turned and
gazed across the field at their goal, a dim outline in
the rapidly fading light.

"Come on," he said. "The snow isn't deep
enough yet to really hinder us, but pretty soon we
won't be able to see that building anymore. Let's
go."

They set off with Barringer in the lead over the
field of stubble, made slick by the new-fallen snow.

He held the lantern up so she could see the path he was carving through the ice crust forming on the snow's surface, and she stumbled in his wake. It wasn't long before Jill was panting. Trudging through the storm was incredibly difficult; she could barely see Barringer's back moving in front of her, and the light he held was a blur. Her feet sank into the stabbing crystals with every step and she felt as if she were being sucked into quicksand. But he trudged on resolutely and, impressed with his determination, she tried her best to keep up with him. When she stumbled once he turned and put his arm around her waist protectively, pulling her along with him. Finally she slipped and fell, and Barringer knelt beside her.

"Are you all right?" he demanded.

"Yes. Just need to…rest for a minute."

"No. No resting, there's no time." He hauled her to her feet as she struggled upward with him.

"Come on," he said, dragging her by her mittened hand.

Jill tried to walk and her legs collapsed.

He shook her roughly, yanking her to her feet at the same time, and Jill realized that he was getting alarmed. She brushed the snow from her face and squared her shoulders.

"Do you want to freeze to death out here?" he barked at her. "I am working on blind instinct at this point, hoping that I remember where that barn was. We have to keep going."

"I can walk," she said, but her frozen feet refused to obey her when she tried to move them.

He set the lantern on the ground and bent to put his arm under her knees. When she realized what he was doing she straightened indignantly and said, "You are not going to carry me."

"Well I'm not going to leave you," he shouted back at her, over the rising wind.

"I can walk," she yelled, wiping her nose with the back of her mitten.

"Then do it!" he shouted.

He took off and then looked back at her. She followed reluctantly, forcing her feet forward step by step with a strength of will she had never known she possessed.

They trudged along, single file, for what seemed like an eternity. Jill's face was freezing, her hands and feet were numb, her legs ached, and she fantasized about the comforts of her bed back in Longmeadow. She had been in this storm forever, she would never get out of it. The flakes flying into her eyes and mouth like moths at a porch light would never stop, they would keep falling forever. The light of Barringer's lantern blurred and she stifled a sob.

Suddenly Barringer turned to her and yelled excitedly, "There it is! Thank God."

Jill peered through the snow and saw nothing but more snow. But she stumbled after him, and when she had gone a few more feet she saw what he was looking at, a barnlike wooden building half con-

cealed by the storm. He set the lantern down and
ran to it, lifting the crossbar that held the door closed
and then shoving the door open.

"Come on!" he yelled, and she hurried in after
him, sagging against the inside wall as he grabbed
the lantern, shut the door again and moved a couple
of crates to prop against it from the inside. He held
the lantern up and gazed around the room.

"Looks like feed and chemical storage for this
farm," he said, his breathing labored, observing the
hemp bags piled against the walls and the shelves
of insecticides and fertilizers.

It was just as cold inside as it was outside; Jill
could see her breath in front of her face in the light
of the lantern. But at least they were protected from
the driving snow and the wind.

Barringer pulled the hood of his jacket down and
set the lantern on an upended crate. "Now, if I can
find some kindling I'll start a fire in that fireplace.
No electricity, but once I get a fire going we'll have
all the comforts of home." He took off his gloves
and rubbed his hands together, then picked up the
lantern again and began to prowl around the shed,
picking up any pieces of cloth or paper he could
find. He had gathered a pile and added some rags to
it when he looked over at Jill.

She was sliding silently down the barn-siding wall
onto the dirt-packed floor.

"Oops," he said, and ran to her side, scooping
her up in his arms. He carried her to a pile of bags
next to the fireplace. Arranging them quickly with

one hand he set her down on them gently and said,
"We're all right now. There's plenty of wood in
here to burn, we'll be fine overnight, and in the
morning we'll get help with the car. Jill? Do you
understand me?"

Jill nodded wearily.

"Good." He unzipped his jacket and put it on top
of her, pulling off her sodden hat and boots also. "I
want to get a fire going, so you just relax and in a
short time it will be warm in here, okay?"

"Okay," she whispered, and he smiled.

"That's my girl," he said, and she wondered how
an offhand endearment from an obviously preoccupied man could have such a salutary effect on her.
She sat up and hugged her knees, watching him as
he stuffed the rags and bits of an old newspaper into
the fireplace, and then added the legs of a discarded
chair. He opened the chimney flue, letting in a blast
of cold air, then lit the last rag from his book of
matches and tossed it on the pile. The fire sputtered
and smoked, then blazed up fiercely. When he had
it going nicely he stripped off his sweatshirt and
spread it out on the floor in front of the fire.

"Come and sit here," he said.

Jill moved obediently and she was soon warm
enough to discard both coats. She looked back at
him and saw that he was selecting empty crates to
dismantle for firewood.

"Still scared?" he said.

"You saved my life," she said.

He put a crate across his knees and started ripping the slats out of it.

"Don't be ridiculous," he answered, grimacing as he worked, dropping a stick at his feet.

"I mean it. I would have stayed out there and frozen solid if you hadn't carried me along with you."

"You always did exaggerate things, Jill. It wasn't nearly as bad as that."

"You said we would freeze to death."

"Look," he said, ripping the last slat out of the box and then tossing the pile of sticks onto the fire, "forget about it. You're not trained for endurance hiking, you could not be expected to hold up like a cross-country skier. We made it here, we're fine, that's the end of the story. In the morning I'll find out who owns this place and pay him for the stuff I'm destroying here and for the use of this shed. Then we'll be on our way back to Longmeadow."

Jill nodded. "All right," she said softly.

He grinned and picked his backpack off the floor. "And guess what's in here. Food."

"You got up early and did that?"

"Actually, I asked Carrie to leave a lunch for us in the fridge and I just took it."

"You're a really good person, you know?" she said softly as he produced a couple of slightly crushed sandwiches, two apples and a bag full of cookies from his pack.

"Eat," he said sternly, handing her an apple.

She took a bite and chewed obediently.

"I filled this thermos at the college. The coffee is pretty old by now but I hope it is still hot." He poured the brew into the cup and handed her the drink.

She started to sip it and he went back to tearing apart crates. He kept adding wood to the fire until it was blazing.

"There," he said finally. "That should last for a few hours before I have to replenish it." He prowled around the shed for a few minutes longer and then said behind her, "Hey, looky here. A metal folding bed with a double mattress. Somewhat old, I'm afraid, but covered with plastic. It will have to do for tonight."

Jill watched him drag the bed from behind a standing shelf and open it up, then drop the striped gray mattress on top of it. He pulled the bed in front of the fire and then spread their coats on top of it.

"Not bad, eh?" he said, surveying his handiwork.

"Don't you ever get tired?" Jill asked wearily. Just watching him drag furniture around after their overland trek enervated her.

"Sure," he said, laughing. "But I can usually keep going until what needs to be done gets done."

"Amen," she said, and put down the thermos cup. She got up and sidled over to the bed, sitting on the edge gingerly and then stretching out full length with a sigh of relief.

"It must be past nine by now. Go to sleep," he said. "In the morning you'll feel much better." He got the lantern and went to the shed's single window, holding the light up to the streaked pane of discolored glass.

"It's still coming down," he said. "Looks like we'll get several inches."

"Hmm-hmm," Jill responded. The warmth of the fire was seeping into her bones, banishing the memory of the biting wind and the freezing snow. Lazily she unzipped her jacket and sat up to take it off, then lay back down and drew it up to her chin like a blanket.

Barringer turned back to see her dozing off and then glanced at his watch. He might as well go to sleep, too. There was nothing to do except keep the fire going until morning. He banked the blaze as high as he could and then lay down next to her, putting his arms around her and adding his coat to hers for warmth. As soon as Jill felt him next to her she turned and snuggled against him, sighing in her sleep and fitting her head into the curve of his shoulder.

Barringer kissed the top of her head and closed his eyes.

In one minute he was sleeping, too.

Jill sat bolt upright and looked around her in terror. The dream was already disintegrating into gray threads of frightening images, but her heart was still pounding.

"Are you all right?" Barringer said, sitting up next to her.

She was so glad to see him she flung herself into

his arms, pushing them both back down on the makeshift bed.

"I think I was dreaming that I was back in the storm," she said, burying her face on his chest.

"No, no," he soothed her, patting her back. "We're safe here, warm and dry. And look, it's morning and the snow has stopped."

They lay prone together for some moments, Jill aware of his strong heartbeat beneath her ear and his slim, muscular frame enfolding hers. She raised her head to look up at him and saw the beard stubble on his jaw, his parted lips, the hazy look of desire in his eyes. When he bent to kiss her his hands slid under her layers of clothing and she felt the electric contact of his warm fingers on her bare skin. Jill was pressing herself to him eagerly when they both heard pounding on the door of the shed.

"Open up in there," a male voice called out ominously. "Westfield Police."

Barringer gestured for Jill to stay put and remain silent as her heart leapt into her throat. He rose and got his revolver and stuck it in the waistband of his pants before removing the crates he had propped against the door when they arrived.

"Right away, Officer," Barringer yelled back as he moved to open the door.

They were confronted by two uniformed police officers who peered into the comparative gloom of the shed from the crisp light of early morning.

"How do you do, Officers?" Barringer said

quickly, stepping forward to offer his hand. "Are we ever glad to see you."

"You folks all right in there?" one of the cops asked. "We found the car abandoned down on the road and this is the only building near it for miles. We figured you were in here when we saw the smoke coming from the chimney."

Barringer explained what had happened while Jill felt her pulse rate dropping slowly. She saw him take the first cop aside and show him some identification during a private conversation, after which the cop's attitude became deferential.

"Young lady, you won't have to walk across that field again," the cop, whose name was Scanlon, said kindly to Jill. "We've radioed for a Ski-Doo and you'll get a ride back to our cruiser."

"Thank you so much," Jill said, sliding off the bed. "Is there any way I can call my father down in Longmeadow? Tony's cell phone wouldn't work out here in the country and my dad must be really worried about us by now."

Scanlon gestured for the second cop to take over this chore, and then Scanlon went back to his conversation with Barringer. Jill was patched through to a phone line and spoke with her relieved father, whose guard then asked to speak to Barringer.

"Ride's here," Scanlon announced, as they heard the roaring of a Ski-Doo in the distance. "Where would you two kids like to go? It's going to be a while before the service can dig your car out and then it may not be running."

"Is there a hotel in the nearest town?" Barringer asked, glancing at Jill.

"Sure, a bed-and-breakfast on Blackberry Road in Westfield. I'll call ahead for you," Scanlon said.

"Uh, can I leave some money for the owners here?" Tony asked as a Ski-Doo with Westfield PD emblazoned on its side pulled up to the door, spraying snow.

"This is Bobby Dearborn's shed, he has the farm here. His house is on the east road. I'll talk to him, there will be no charge."

"Are you sure?" Barringer asked, gesturing to the shambles he had made of the shed. "I busted up the place pretty good."

"I'll take care of it," Scanlon said to him, and made a dismissive gesture.

Jill understood suddenly that they were playing cops and robbers and Scanlon was local law enforcement cooperating with the FBI.

"Hop on, miss," the patrolman on the Ski-Doo said.

Jill climbed on behind him and was transported across the snow as if she were flying on a magic carpet. In the poststorm sunlight the blanket of snow blazed brightly and she enjoyed the ride. When they got back to the road Jill was left with the patrolman's partner, Scanlon's cruiser, the UV that had brought the Ski-Doo, and her ditched car. She sat in the warm cruiser with the new cop and drank his too strong coffee while everybody came back from the shed. When Barringer slipped in beside her in the back seat he squeezed her shoulder and winked.

Jill smiled and then looked away from him, a tightness growing in her throat.

What was she going to do when he left?

They said their goodbyes to their rescuers and the two patrolmen drove them to the Blackberry Inn, where the hostess-owner was waiting for them.

Mrs. Halstrom was a sixtyish matron with styled white hair, a checked housedress and an officious air.

"What a terrible thing to happen, get stranded in a freak storm like that," Mrs. Holstrom said, as she led them up the stairs of her colonial establishment to the bedrooms on the second floor. "It's much too early for a heavy snow. Mike Scanlon told me he was afraid he would be reporting a couple of deaths."

They trudged behind her, nodding. She didn't seem to require replies, so they let her talk as she showed them to two adjoining rooms that connected through a door in the shared wall.

"Mike told me you aren't married so I gave you two rooms. You probably think that's old-fashioned of me, but I just feel that hostelries should have standards. Now, room service runs all day until 6:00 p.m., mealtimes in the dining room are posted on the board outside the door. Do you think you'll want some breakfast?"

She turned and faced them. Both of them stared at her and shook their heads in unison.

"All right, then," she said, unlocking their doors and giving them the keys. "Mike said he would call later with a report on your car. The red button on the phone rings at the desk."

They both watched her go and then looked at each other.

"I think I'll take a shower," Jill said quietly.

"I'll be right next door," Barringer replied.

Jill went into her room. Barringer followed her inside to check it out briefly.

"Keep the door locked," he said to Jill, then went into his room.

Jill sat in a chair that faced a window overlooking the back lawn and gazed around her. The yellow chintz drapes matched the yellow chintz bedspread and the grass print in the chintz matched the moss green rug. Cherry Queen Anne tables and bedroom suite completed the picture, but Jill was not in the mood to appreciate the setting. She felt filthy to the limit of her imagination and couldn't think of anything beyond getting clean. She stood up and stripped, dropping the clothes on the floor where she stood, and went into the sea-green tiled bathroom. She turned the shower on full force and waited until it was pouring steam, then unwrapped the midget toiletries in the wicker guest basket. She brushed her teeth and then took the soap and shampoo in with her, using up the tiny bottle of shampoo and wearing the soap bar down to a thin sliver before she was done. By the time she turned the water off she felt like a human being again.

Jill wrapped a towel around her torso and picked up the courtesy hair dryer, taking it into the bedroom and plugging it into the wall. It blew a faint tepid breath on her soaking hair, never reaching her scalp. She abandoned that effort and was towel-drying her hair when she heard knocking on the adjoining door.

"Jill, let me in," Barringer said.

Jill glanced back toward the guest robe hanging inside the bathroom, then ignored it and walked to the door. She pulled it open and watched Barringer's expression transform when he saw her.

He had cleaned up also; he was smooth-shaven and wearing a new shirt he had gotten from somewhere.

"Are you all right?" he asked.

"I am now," she said softly.

"Did you miss me?" he said, smiling.

"Oh, Tony," she said, feeling the sting of tears behind her eyes. She was ridiculously glad to see him, considering that he had been gone all of half an hour.

He pulled her into his arms.

"I think I am falling for you," he said huskily, his lips against her ear. "I just thought you should know that."

The towel she was wearing slipped to the floor and he held her away to look at her. His gaze consumed her.

"You are so beautiful," he whispered, enfolding her again, running his palms down her sides, feeling the warmth of her body crushed to his. "You are everything I have ever wanted, right here in my arms.''

Jill closed her eyes as he pulled her damp hair back and kissed the side of her neck, supporting her weight as they crossed the short distance to the bed. They fell on the coverlet together as his mouth slid along the curve of her shoulder, then up her throat, then came to rest on her lips in a masterful kiss that told Jill that this time he would not be diverted.

By anything.

He moved on top of her and fitted his body to hers as she arched against him, falling under the spell of his caresses. She had never been kissed the way he kissed her; his confidence and desire left no room for resistance, she was swept away as soon as his mouth found hers. His arm, with muscles tensed, slipped around her waist and he rolled her slightly away from him, finding her breast with his free hand. He raised one nipple to a pebble-hard bud, running his thumb over the sensitive flesh until it dimpled and rose in response. Then he sucked on it, delicately at first, then with increasing intensity until she was moaning, locking her bare legs around his jeans-clad hips. He covered the other breast with his palm as Jill sank her fingers into his hair. She felt him hard and heavy against her, the denim of his pants rubbing her bare flesh. She wanted him naked, too, and when he raised his head and looked at her, his eyes half closed dreamily, she whispered, ''Take off your clothes.''

He released her and stood at her command, unbuttoning his shirt rapidly and tossing it on the rug as he kicked off his shoes. He never took his gaze from hers as he unbuckled his belt and unzipped his jeans. He took off his ankle holster and set it on the nightstand beside the bed. Jill's gaze drank in his lean torso and flat abdomen as he dropped his pants and came toward her, discarding his underwear and socks as he lay down with her.

When he embraced her fully again she gasped at the contact, then sighed with satisfaction as the feeling of his bare body against hers responded to an emptiness within her that had longed to be filled. She wound her arms around his neck and kissed him fervently everywhere she could reach, his shoulders, his chest, touching the tip of her tongue to his small flat nipples and then running her tongue down to his navel. His breath hissed between his teeth and he fell back, allowing her greater access. She indulged her every daydream and fantasy about him, licking her way across his hip, pressing her burning cheek to his belly, then reaching for him as he closed his eyes and groaned helplessly. She stroked him, touching and exploring. She saw him put his forearm over his eyes as waves of pleasure passed over his face. Finally he sat up and grabbed her hand.

"Stop!" he gasped, holding her fingers fast in his own.

"What is it?" Jill asked. "Don't you like it?"

He laughed shortly and rolled over on the bed, facedown. "No, I like it just fine. Come here." He pulled her down next to him and said, "Don't you realize what you were doing to me?'' He traced one of her eyebrows with his forefinger lazily.

''I just wanted to…well, no. I guess I didn't realize. I've never done this before.''

His face changed. ''You've never done what before?''

''Made love.''

''You mean you're a…?''

''Virgin? You can say the word. Yes.''

He sat up on the edge of the bed and stared at the floor. ''You wait until now to tell me this?'' he asked incredulously.

''What? You don't want me anymore because I'm a virgin?''

''Don't be ridiculous. I've wanted you from the first moment I saw you, nothing is going to change that. But I thought surely a former boyfriend or somebody along the way…you're so pretty.''

''Would you feel better if I had slept with the Eighth Army before I met you?''

He closed his eyes and shook his head. ''Of course not. It's just such a responsibility, to be the first.''

''Oh, and you don't want that responsibility? Why? Will it make it more difficult for you to leave me when you're through with this 'assignment'?'' She jumped off the bed but had not gone more than two steps before he leapt up and tackled her.

''Stop putting words in my mouth,'' he said in her ear, lifting her off her feet as she kicked and flailed her arms. He set her down on the bed and fell on top of her, pinning her under him by holding each of her wrists in one of his hands at her shoulder level.

"You're hurting my wrists!" she hissed.

"No, I'm not," he replied equably.

"How do you know?" she demanded irritably.

"I can use several holds that will keep an opponent immobilized without inflicting any pain or physical damage. This is one of them. Would you like me to demonstrate the others?"

"Save it for another 'opponent,'" she said.

She turned her head to escape his penetrating gaze and he said, "Look at me."

She gazed back at him defiantly. His eyes were three inches from hers, shot with gold spikes around the green iris and fringed by impossibly long lashes.

"I want this to be a good experience for you and the first time, well, it's not always…"

"Fun?" Jill suggested archly, relaxing as she realized that his concern was for her rather than for himself. "I sure was having a good time so far."

He smiled and kissed the tip of her nose. "It may be uncomfortable," he said gently.

"I know that."

"I just don't want to hurt you," he added quietly.

She put her hand up to touch his cheek. "You couldn't," she whispered. "I trust you."

He turned his head to kiss her fingers and then bent his head and tongued her collarbone, beginning to make love to her again.

Jill sighed, letting her head fall back on the pillow. He kissed and caressed her slowly, repeatedly, teasingly, moving down her body until her hands were tangled in his damp hair and she was moaning steadily. Her entire body was dewed with perspiration, and as he kissed her thighs her legs moved restlessly.

"What do you want?" he whispered, his face flushed, his skin on fire, his mouth hot and wet against her. He dragged his lips through the golden mound at the apex of her thighs and her legs fell apart.

"Tell me," he said, kissing the inside of her thigh and slipping one hand between her legs. She whimpered and pressed against him, her breathing audible.

"Touch me," she sighed, groaning deeply as he obeyed, stroking her until she put her hand to her mouth to stifle her sounds of gratification. Then she arched toward him when he put his arms around her hips and lifted her to his mouth.

Jill gasped and started when she felt his tongue invade her softest, most secret parts, but he persisted and she soon went limp with pleasure. She dropped her hands to his shoulders and dug her nails into his skin as he caressed her with his lips and tongue. Jill felt herself rushing upward, ever upward, as he pushed her toward the peak. She drowned in warmth, crying out for him, as she finally shuddered and then lay still, spent, her eyes closed. Her fingers roamed through his hair, now so damp with sweat that it was clinging to his head. He lay with his cheek against her leg, his eyes closed also, but so excited that he knew he would have to hold back somehow and go slowly when he took her. Barringer was lost, more emotionally intoxicated than he had ever been by a woman; he could not stop now.

"I want you," he murmured, moving up to lie next to her on the bed. "So much."

Her eyes opened and she smiled, reaching out to touch his cheek. "I want you, too," she whispered. "I want to feel you inside me."

He pulled her into his arms and shifted her under him, easing her into position as she hooked her slim legs around his hips and buried her face against his damp, hot shoulder. His whole body was in readiness: his arms taut, his thigh muscles tensed, his feet braced against the bed. She felt his weight pressing her down and his manhood heavy against her leg, then the pressure of his entry.

She gasped and he paused as he felt resistance, closing his eyes and biting his lower lip, quelling the overpowering urge to bear down and continue. Jill's body tensed under his and he felt her fingernails digging into his upper arms. He lifted his head and waited for Jill to look up at him.

"Okay?" he said.

She nodded.

"Should I stop?" It took all of his willpower to force himself to ask the question.

"Don't stop," she said. "I want this with you." She ran her hands down his back, feeling the muscles tighten as she touched them, the spray of curling hair on his chest rough against her breasts. "I want you to be the one."

"I'll try...to go slow," he said through clenched teeth, pushing again as she went rigid beneath him.

He eased forward gently, beads of sweat breaking out anew on his forehead, then paused to kiss her lingeringly. Her mouth opened under his and she relaxed, reaching up to caress him, lifting his hair off his forehead and running her fingers along the shell of his ear.

"You can go a little faster," she said.

He tried again, gasping aloud with the effort of restraining his impulse to plunge into her, and he could feel her enclosing him slightly as she gasped and turned her head.

Jill said something thickly but her mouth was pressed to his shoulder and he could not understand it.

"What?" he panted.

"More," she said.

He sank into her fully and groaned helplessly with the sensation. She stiffened slightly, then settled back and dug her heels into the backs of his legs. He pushed up and sank again, and this time she made a guttural sound that echoed his own, closing her eyes.

Barringer felt a surge of triumph and bent his head to kiss her again. She looked into his eyes as he did so and then let him see her pleasure when he moved inside her again.

Barringer closed his eyes and carried them both along on a wave of sensation.

Everything was going to be fine, he thought, as Jill cried out and then relaxed as he brought her to completion.

He was in love with Jill Darcy. But he couldn't tell her that.

Not while he was spying on her father.

Jill stirred first and slid off the bed, lifting Barringer's arm from her torso gently and replacing it on the sheet. She went into the bathroom and took another quick shower; she was bleeding slightly and a purple bruise was showing on her thigh, but she had never been happier.

She was a woman now, and in love.

The world was bright with promise.

She belted the guest robe around her and went back into the bedroom to find Barringer sitting on the edge of the bed, watching her.

"Are you all right?" he asked.

"Never better," she replied, sitting next to him and putting her head on his bare shoulder.

"Do you love me?" he asked soberly.

"I love you."

His arm came around her. "Good. Are you sure you aren't in pain?"

"I am not in pain. But I am hungry. Didn't Mrs. Halstrom say room service ran until six?"

He fell back on the bed in feigned surprise. "Send up a flare, a new world order has been declared.

She's hungry.'' He rolled over and produced a plastic-bound loose-leaf notebook from the top drawer of the nightstand, flipping through it idly. ''Ah, here we go. Order anything you like, Uncle Sam is paying the tab.'' He tossed the book to her.

''Oh, you do it. I don't feel like talking to anybody but you.''

''Sorry, but I'm not supposed to be in here, remember? We wouldn't want to shatter Mrs. Halstrom's illusions.''

Jill stuck her tongue out at him and picked up the book.

''Order a lot of stuff so I can have some,'' he added.

She stared at him. ''And what? You're going to hide and then gobble everything?''

''That was my plan,'' he said, and smiled.

Jill examined the offerings and then called the kitchen and placed a large room service order.

''Sounds like enough for five,'' Barringer commented as she hung up the phone.

She flung herself on top of him. ''I intend to work you very hard,'' she said, and he sighed.

''This is always what happens,'' he said wearily. ''One time with me and they're insatiable.''

'' 'They're?' Who is 'they'? Exactly how many women have you been with?'' she asked worriedly. She got up and moved away from him.

''Oh, Jill, I don't know,'' he replied evasively, realizing that he had said the wrong thing. ''It was a joke.''

"Well, give me a round number, a guess. Am I just one of a teeming horde?" Would he get bored with her and move on? Was her inexperience a novelty, a quirk that would lose its luster for him quickly? Was she destined to be alone again once she was dismissed as just another notch on his belt?

"No, of course not." He stood and came around to her side of the bed. When he sat next to her she edged away from him.

He stood and threw his hands up in exasperation.

"You have to help me here, you're driving me crazy," he said. "First I am a cad because I hesitated to deflower a virgin, and now I am a cad because I didn't hesitate enough in the past? You can't have it both ways, Jill, which is it to be?"

Jill was silent, anxious and confused.

"I haven't lived your rarefied life, Jill," he added quietly. "Some of the women in my past were mistakes, some were using me or used by me, only a few meant anything. Quantity is not quality, believe me, and there weren't nearly as many as you seem to imagine." He knelt before her and took both of her hands in his, raising her fingers to his lips and kissing them. "I never felt about any of them the way I feel about you, and that's the truth."

Jill freed one of her hands and touched his cheek. "I'm sorry. I guess I'm a little insecure. The last day or so has been overwhelming. I am feeling so many emotions—happiness and contentment and joy, but I'm still just a little scared, too."

"There is no reason to be scared." He climbed

up onto the bed with her and embraced her, kissing her tenderly, and then beginning anew his exploration of her body. "I am with you, I don't want anybody else. Put all of those thoughts right out of your mind."

Jill sighed and succumbed to his caresses, reaching for him and encircling him with her fingers as his mouth moved over her body. He groaned and fell on his back, pulling her on top of him.

"Come on to me," he said thickly, and she straddled him, gasping aloud as she climbed astride him and then dropping her head to his shoulder, overcome with pleasure.

"Yes?" he muttered, as she began to rock against him.

"Oh, yes," she whispered, shuddering delicately as he guided her hip movements with his hands.

They moved sinuously together to a quick resolution, and Jill had just collapsed in his arms when a knock came at the door.

"Room service," Mrs. Halstrom's voice announced.

Barringer feigned an expression of comic horror and disengaged himself, scrambling around on the bed and floor for his clothes. Then he stood and held one finger to his lips dramatically, like a character in a silent movie.

"Idiot," Jill said, laughing.

He opened the door to his room and made a sweeping bow as he went through it, dropping his shirt in the process. He grabbed the shirt and pulled the door closed behind him as Jill belted the guest robe around her. She glanced around the room, shoved Barringer's gun under the pillow and went to answer the door.

"Hi, Mrs. Halstrom," Jill said, as her hostess wheeled a cart full of covered metal dishes and rattling silverware into the room.

"You've got enough to feed an army here," Mrs. Halstrom observed, glancing toward the connecting door.

"I didn't realize that you were such a jack of all trades," Jill observed quickly. "You do room service, too?" She turned to clear a space before the bed for the trolley and her breath stopped when she saw Barringer's jockey shorts on the rug. With a swift kick she sent them sailing under the bed and then dropped the spread to the floor.

"I brought the food myself because I have a message from Turner's Garage," Mrs. Halstrom said. "Your car wasn't damaged and it should be ready to go around two o'clock."

Jill wondered why the woman hadn't put the call through to Tony's room, and then realized that bringing the message gave Mrs. Halstrom an excuse to check out what was going on upstairs.

Jill smiled. If she only knew.

"Thanks so much, I think I can take it from here," Jill said pointedly, and with a final glance around the room Mrs. Halstrom departed, reluctantly.

The door to Barringer's room opened a crack.

"Is the coast clear?" he hissed, coming into her room. He had donned his jeans but was still barefoot and his shirt was open down the front, sleeves rolled to the elbow.

Jill got down on her hands and knees and fished his underwear out to display for him on one extended finger.

He grinned. "Did she see them?"

Jill stared at him balefully.

His mouth fell open in feigned shock. "Did you tell her they were yours?"

Jill threw the shorts at him and they landed on his bare shoulder. He left them there and made straight for the room service cart, where he uncovered and seized a cheeseburger and took a huge bite of it, closing his eyes in bliss.

"American cuisine, the fuel of the heartland," he said, sighing. "Nothing quite like it." He sat on the edge of the bed, chewing energetically.

"Where did you get that shirt?" Jill asked, pulling a chair up to sit across the cart from him.

"Mrs. Halstrom has a shop down on the first floor, around the corner from the reception desk, where she overcharges her patrons for the necessaries of life. I suspect that there aren't too many merchandising opportunities that escape her."

"It's a little big."

"This was the closest to my size that I could get. Mrs. Halstrom seems to favor large sizes."

"Or maybe that's what was left," Jill said. "Just don't let her alter it while you're wearing it."

He shot her an arch glance, took another bite of his burger, then downed a huge gulp of his drink.

"Gah," he said, making a face. "What is this? Iced tea?"

"Yes, iced tea, is that all right with you?"

"Doesn't this place have any soda?"

"The proprietor apparently does not stock it."

"Mrs. Halstrom just climbed a couple of notches higher on my hit list," Barringer intoned darkly. "What do you say we come back here on our first anniversary and tie her to a chair, then beat the local gossip out of her?"

Jill's heart jumped sideways in her chest. This was the first reference he had ever made to marriage.

"Sounds like a plan," she said lightly.

"I'm sure she knows what Scanlon *really* does on his early morning rounds," Barringer added, popping a potato chip into his mouth.

"Tony," Jill said soberly.

He looked at her. "Yes?"

"What are you going to do about us?"

"Us?"

"You and me, your job, your assignment, all of it."

He put his burger down. "I don't know."

She studied him across the room service cart.

He shrugged. "I have to do something. I can't just go on..." He stopped abruptly.

"Sleeping with me?" Jill suggested delicately.

He nodded. "...and pretending that everything is going smoothly with my assignment."

"Actually, you could," Jill said.

He raised his brows.

"Who would know the difference?" Jill asked.

"I would," he said.

"Oh, for heaven's sake. Do you have to be so damned noble? If I don't tell them, and you don't tell them, no one will know. You could wrap this whole thing up without anyone ever suspecting we were together before it ended! No harm, no foul."

"I am going to tell them."

Jill stood up and put her hands on her hips. "Why?"

He sat forward, clasping his hands together. "Jill, listen to me. This isn't like pricking your finger when you're twelve and promising always to be best friends with the kid next door. I took oaths, I swore on Bibles. Fifty other guys tried for the FBI position I got! I can't just disregard all that."

"I'm sorry," Jill said quietly. "I understand, I really do. It's just that I'm...uncertain. Maybe I'm afraid that your job is more important to you than I am."

He got up and put his arms around her tightly. "I knew what I was getting into when I made the choice today to be with you. I had thought about it almost from the time I met you and I always knew the consequences. Now, if that causes me to separate from the bureau, I accept that. With the experience I have there are lots of other things I can do. But I'm not going to sneak around about it. I'm going to lay my cards on the table and see what happens. I won't do anything else.''

Jill lifted her chin from his shoulder and smiled tremulously. ''If I wasn't so worried I know I would be proud of you,'' she said.

''That's not necessary,'' he said lightly. ''Just as long as you're never ashamed of me.''

He was letting go of her as the bedside phone rang.

''It's my new policy never to answer phones,'' he said.

''It's probably about the car,'' Jill said. ''Mrs. Halstrom said it would be ready at two.''

She walked over to it and picked up the receiver. Jill listened and then said, ''Fine,'' and hung up.

''What?'' Barringer said.

''Mrs. Halstrom wanted to let us know that check-out time is noon,'' Jill told him.

''Gee, I never would have guessed. It's posted about six places in this room and twice in the bathroom.''

''I think she suspects something 'unmarried' is going on up here. She was very anxious to tell me about the car.''

''Well, we're out of here.'' Barringer went into his room and returned with his backpack and a paper bag.

''I got these for you at Halstrom's shop when I bought my shirt. They may not fit well but they're clean.''

"Thanks," Jill said warmly, accepting the slacks and sweater gratefully.

Barringer started jamming items into his pack as Jill got dressed in the clothes he had given her. He fastened his ankle holster and buttoned his shirt as she fluffed pillows, pulled the disarranged spread back onto the bed and tidied up around him.

"There's nothing more to do in my room," Barringer said, slinging his pack onto his back and picking up his coat. "So let's go."

Jill paused to look around and he said, "What is it?"

"I want to remember it," she said simply, and he leaned over to kiss her cheek.

"Come on," he said. "Before Mrs. Halstrom shows up with a few more questions."

Their hostess fidgeted all through the bill-paying process and examined Barringer's credit card as if he had handed her Confederate money. If she had known that the number on it was an account for federal employees their departure might have been a lot more interesting than it was.

They walked the three blocks to the garage through frozen snow and refrozen slush and claimed the car, which looked unchanged despite its recent ordeal.

Jill felt very changed from the last time she had been in it.

Barringer looked over at her as they settled in and he pulled out into the icy street.

"Are you ready to go back home and face...well, everything?" he asked her.

"Do I have a choice?"

"No."

"I wish we could have stayed at the Blackberry Inn forever," Jill said.

"With Mrs. Halstrom following you into the bathroom? I don't think so."

"She'll miss us," Jill said, and he laughed.

"She's probably going over the rooms with a fingerprint kit right now," Barringer added.

"I hope I never become dried up and bitter and nosy, living my life through other people," Jill said sadly.

"Stick with me, kid, and you'll never get old."

"Who are you? Peter Pan?"

"I'm the next best thing, the man who just made love to you. And that will keep you young."

The afternoon lengthened as they drove home, and by the time they reached the Darcy house it was almost dark. Barringer shifted his gun to his waistband and walked ahead of Jill to check out the porch and front lawn as they walked into the house.

Arthur Darcy was in the front hall, his glasses pushed up into his graying hair, his arms folded combatively.

"Well, young man," he said, staring down his aquiline nose at Barringer. "Would you mind telling me what you've been up to with my daughter?"

Chapter 7

Jill opened her mouth to intervene but Barringer held up his hand to silence her. At the same instant the cell phone in his jacket pocket began to ring.

He sighed with exasperation and pulled the phone out, yanking the antenna up forcefully.

"Excuse me, please, I know this is the worst timing but I have to take this now," he said to them, and stepped into the dining room, shutting the door to the hall.

Arthur Darcy looked at his daughter, who looked back at him defiantly.

"Have you anything to say to me?" Darcy asked.

"I think I'll wait for Tony to come back before we discuss it," Jill said.

"Oh, it's Tony now, is it?" Darcy said, raising his brows.

In the dining room Barringer hit the respond button and said "Barringer here," but instead of getting an answer he saw a code number flash on his screen, then repeat. He lowered the antenna on the phone and put it back in his pocket, his expression thoughtful.

The number was 431. It meant that he had to go immediately to a PO box in Longmeadow that had been set up for him as an emergency contact. A written message would be waiting for him there, the content of which the bureau did not want to trust to the cell phone system.

The code had not been used previously on this assignment, and he wondered what the message was.

But right now he had to get past Jill's irate father in order to make it to the post office.

He opened the door to the hall and both Darcys turned to look at him, wearing identical inquisitive expressions.

"I have to go out for a short while," he said.

Jill sighed and her father looked mutinous.

"Mr. Darcy, this is my job and I have to do it," Barringer said. "What I can tell you for now is that I care for your daughter very much and when I have a chance to explain everything that happened over the past couple of days I think you will be satisfied with what I have to say."

Jill stared at Barringer, her face growing warm, and Arthur Darcy looked ambushed.

"I'll be back as soon as possible," Barringer said, zipping up his coat and dashing through the front door. "Mr. Darcy, your guard is on duty in the car across the street, so if you both stay here until I get back you will be fine."

Jill and her father exchanged glances. Then Arthur threw up his hands and stalked back upstairs.

Jill went into the living room and sat down on the sofa to wait for Tony.

The Darcy car skidded to a stop in front of the Longmeadow post office and Barringer got out, stepping into a snowbank and then stamping out of it. Regular hours were over but the lobby was open, and he took his key ring out as he entered the room lined with cubbyhole metal boxes, the marble floor stained and muddy from the recent storm. He unlocked the box that matched his key number and snatched the envelope that lay inside. He looked around quickly—he was alone. He ripped it open and read quickly: "All investigation of subject A. R. Darcy is to cease immediately. Informant located elsewhere. Assignment going forward is to be protection for Darcy family only."

It was signed with the identification number of his superior at the FBI.

Barringer leaned against the wall and closed his eyes. He opened them and read the message once more, then let out a whoop that echoed eerily in the empty lobby.

Arthur was cleared. No more sneaking around trying to prove something that couldn't be proved, no more deceiving Jill about his own dual purpose in

her house. It was a gift, a reprieve, a sign that all
would be well. He didn't have to lie to Jill anymore.
She would never know that he had been investigat-
ing her father and that alone was cause for celebra-
tion.

But there soon would be another one. He had
spotted a jewelry store that was still open on the
main street. Stuffing the note in his back jeans
pocket he closed the PO box and locked it. Then he
sprinted for the door and ran down the snow-laden
street, bounding through the entrance to the jewelry
store as the thirtyish female clerk inside looked
pointedly at the clock.

"We close at six," she said.

"I want to buy an engagement ring," Barringer
announced.

When Barringer came back into the Darcy house
Jill was waiting for him in the living room. He went
over to her, pulled her to her feet and hugged her
fiercely.

"Get dressed up," he said to her. "We are going
out on the town." He took her by the hand and
twirled her in a circle.

She stared at him, aghast. "What are you talking
about? It's too late to make a reservation, not to
mention that things have slowed to a crawl due to
the storm."

"That's exactly why we should be able to get in
anywhere," he said. "All the sensible people will

be staying home.'' He kissed her loudly on the cheek.

"What are we celebrating?'' she asked, laughing.

"Life, love, the upcoming winter solstice. Who needs a reason to celebrate?''

Jill sobered for a second. "Tony! The cops didn't find the people who have been harassing us, did they?''

He looked at her, then looked away. "No. I wish I could say that they have. But I'm sure that will happen soon, and in the meantime we are going on a date. An honest-to-goodness, 1950s, Archie-and-Veronica-type date.''

Jill giggled, caught up in his infectious mood.

"Where's your father?'' Barringer asked abruptly. "I have to talk to him.''

"I think you'd better wait with that, Tony. He got a call from the school and then went into his study, saying that he didn't want to be disturbed.''

"I really should explain to him…''

"It'll keep,'' Jill said, interrupting. "I think your passionate declaration of affection for me allayed his fears that you were taking advantage of his little girl.''

Barringer pushed her hair back from her face and kissed her forehead.

"Go and get dressed,'' he said, removing his coat. "What's your favorite restaurant in town?''

"Uh, Il Sol, I guess. It's on Delancey Street.''

"I'll call and see if they can take us.'' He turned to put his coat on a chair and the trailing sleeve dragged a folded slip of paper from his jeans pocket onto the floor.

They both looked at it.

"What's that?" Jill asked.

"Oh, just a grocery list," he said, not meeting her eyes, snatching it up and shoving it back into his pocket.

Jill watched him curiously. The sheet was cream bond, hardly the type of paper people used for shopping lists, and he had the same guilty expression he had worn the night she had found him operating Arthur's computer.

For somebody whose business was subterfuge, he was a terrible liar.

What exactly was going on? she wondered. Why would he lie about something so mundane? She filed the question away for future references and said, "Give me some time to get ready. Make the reservation for eight."

"Will do," he said, going to the phone in the kitchen.

Jill ran upstairs and rifled through her closet, selecting a sweater and skirt combination in navy that looked a little dressy, adding gold earrings and a chain. She found pantyhose and pumps, sprayed herself with perfume and brushed her hair until it crackled. She pulled it up into a topknot, grabbed her purse and was ready.

Barringer was waiting for her, dressed in the suit he had worn to the mixer.

"You look lovely," Barringer said, his eyes lighting up at the sight of her.

"Thank you."

"I told your father that we were going out and he had to stay home," Barringer added. "His guard will stay in place outside. I also said that I would give him all the details of our recent trip whenever he wanted. We have an appointment to talk tomorrow."

"Am I invited?" Jill asked, as he helped her into her coat and then donned his.

"No. This is man-to-man stuff, and I'll handle it," Barringer said confidently.

Jill was sure that he would.

Snow from the piles on either side of the walkway blew across their path and sprayed into their faces as they walked to the car. Barringer had started the car and it was warm inside when he helped her over a snowbank and into the passenger seat.

Il Sol was a short distance away and the parking lot was empty when they arrived.

The walk to the entrance had been blown clean of snow. They passed under a green metal trellis and went into the restaurant. The dining room to their left was carpeted in red. Gold sconces shed light on the silk-covered walls and the standing plants were strung with tiny white lights. A well-stocked bar extended along one mirrored wall, and a woman in a black cocktail dress was sitting at a white baby grand piano, playing softly.

The maître d' approached them.

"Your choice of tables, sir," he said to Barringer, who gestured to one near the piano.

They entered the dining room to find one couple seated at another table nearby and the staff hovering. The maître d' sat them and gave them large, gold-tasseled menus. A barman arrived shortly to take their drink orders.

"Two champagne cocktails, please," Barringer said. The man nodded and walked away.

"So we are celebrating something more than the winter solstice?" Jill said.

"Yes."

"What?"

"Us," he said.

As the waiter brought a basket of bread, a man in a black tuxedo entered from a side door and leaned on the piano. The pianist played an introduction to "O Sole Mio," and the man began to sing.

Barringer and Jill looked at each other. The guy had the loudest singing voice Jill had ever heard. They endured the song, not speaking because it was not possible to do so while the song lasted. When the singer reached an especially earsplitting crescendo Barringer got up and said directly into Jill's ear, "I'll see what I can do about this."

Jill watched as Barringer went to stand by the piano. He waited until the singer had finished and then put his hand on the tenor's shoulder, steering him away from the accompanist. They had a short conversation, and the next thing Jill knew the tenor was taking off his dark jacket and having a drink with the bartender at the bar.

"What did you say to him?" Jill asked as Barringer returned to their table.

"I told him that we wanted to have a quiet conversation and I would pay him double what he is making for singing tonight if he just left us in peace. The owner isn't here this evening so he took me up on it. The cashier is running my card through for his payment now."

"Tony, you didn't! Was he insulted?"

"Not at all. He seemed glad to get the night off."

Jill chuckled at his audacity. Never in her life would she have had the nerve to do something similar, no matter how much the "entertainment" annoyed her.

"Now, where were we?" Barringer asked as the waiter arrived to take their orders. When he finally departed Barringer sighed dramatically and said, "To think I brought you here so that we could have a quiet, intimate dinner. I would have been better off taking you to Grand Central Station. There are only ten other people in this place tonight, including the cook in the kitchen. How can they be so intrusive? I'm expecting Mrs. Halstrom to show up any minute with a bill for toothpaste and a lecture on forbidden fornication in hotel rooms."

Jill was struggling not to laugh. He was trying so hard to make this evening live up to some romantic image he had in his mind, and in his estimation failing miserably.

The waiter brought their salads and from then on they were left pretty much alone, except for service people changing plates and filling glasses. Barringer relaxed and talked easily and Jill realized that this was the happiest she had ever seen him. He had always been on his guard with her, to a greater or lesser extent, and this was the first time she was seeing his "civilian" personality. She had seen him in a crisis and she had seen him handling difficult situations, but this was the Tony who made jokes and told stories and had a real life. And she liked him. A lot. She loved him.

"So maybe we can do that?" he said as the waiter served their desserts.

"Hmm?" Jill replied, smiling at him.

He put his fork down and eyed her skeptically. "You haven't been listening to a word I've said, have you?"

Jill looked sheepish. "I guess not. I have just been studying you and thinking how handsome you are."

He narrowed his eyes. "Compliments will not get you off the hook, miss."

"I mean it. When I first met you I could not take my eyes off you. I thought surely you would know."

"All I knew was that you didn't care to have me around. You made that very clear," he said dryly.

"I wanted you so badly," she whispered, holding his gaze with hers. "I thought about you, fantasized about you, dreamed about you. When you touched me I went hot and cold at once, when you kissed me that night at Granny's I was totally smitten. I couldn't think about anything else for days.''

He was very still, listening to her, enraptured by her précis of her love for him, the first time he had ever heard it described from her point of view.

''Neither could I,'' he finally said, clearing his throat. ''Which reminds me...'' he added, and pulled a white satin box out of his pocket. He put it on the table between them.

''For you,'' he said.

Breathless, she reached for it.

''Open it,'' he said.

Jill did, and gasped. She looked up at him. ''Does this mean what I think it means?'' she murmured.

''Yes. I am asking you, however awkwardly, to marry me.''

She stared at him. ''But...but...we can't get married.''

He sighed and closed his eyes. ''Jill, you aren't following the script here. When I ask you to marry me you are supposed to scream with joy and throw yourself into my arms.''

Jill smiled gently. ''I'm sorry, of course I want to marry you. But you said that once you tell your superiors about us that you would be fired and then forbidden to see me....''

''How can they forbid me to see my wife?'' he asked.

Jill gazed back at him.

''Sure, they'll drop me once I tell them about us, but even the FBI can't order me to abandon my wife. I'll present them with a fait accompli—a marriage. They won't be happy, but there will be nothing they can do about it.''

"Except fire you."

He nodded. "But I can get another job easily. Ex bureau operatives are in demand in law enforcement, corporate security, private detection, plenty of fields."

"Even ex FBI men with no references?"

"It is not unusual for people to leave the bureau without letters of recommendation," he said dryly.

"Why?"

"It's a hard life, demanding of time and devotion, and if you step an inch out of line they drop you. Everyone involved in the community knows that."

"What community?"

"Espionage, security, whatever you want to call it. I'll say I worked for the bureau, and if a prospective employer checks on that the bureau will confirm it and my period of service. Separation terms will not be discussed."

"You were so certain that you wanted to do everything right," Jill lamented.

"And that hasn't changed. I will tell them everything, be aboveboard just as I said. I will explain exactly how it all happened and tender my resignation. The only difference will be that if we are married they can't stop me from seeing you."

"What about school, my job on campus?" she asked.

"We'll get a place near here so you can finish.

I'll get a job locally. You'll be living with me so you'll be out of danger. My partner will continue with your father until they catch whoever is behind the harassment.''

Jill searched his face, wanting to believe him.

"Look, I have some money saved," he said, "enough to live on for a while until we get settled. I promise you that it will be all right."

Jill's eyes filled with tears. "I don't care about money, Tony."

"So what's your answer?" he said, smiling.

"Of course I'll marry you," Jill said, wiping her eyes with her thumb. "Did you think I would say no?"

"You had me worried for a minute there." He leaned over and palmed the box, taking the ring out and slipping it on her finger. It glowed and winked in the restaurant light like a sparkler.

"We're officially engaged," he said. "The engagement should last about five minutes, since I want to get married as soon as possible. Then I can leave the bureau and we can get on with our lives."

"You have no doubts about leaving?" Jill asked softly. "The service has been your home for so long, and all that talk of oaths and Bibles... I know it meant a lot to you."

"You're my home now," he replied. "If I have to make a choice, I choose you. No job or career could ever take precedence over you in my life."

"But it was through your job that you met me."

"And for that I am grateful. It doesn't mean I'll

allow my job to dictate the terms of the rest of my life. All I want now is to separate from the service honorably and be with you.''

"I hope you never have cause to regret what you gave up for me," Jill said quietly.

"I know I won't," he replied.

The waiter arrived and looked at their untouched desserts.

"More coffee?" he said pointedly.

"No, thanks," Barringer said. "We'll take the check, please."

The waiter went off to tabulate the bill as Jill asked curiously, "Where and when did you get this ring? I know I wasn't with you at the time."

"At a jeweler's this afternoon when I went out."

"Oh, after that mystery phone call when we arrived back home? I thought that was company business."

"It was, but I fit in a personal errand," he said quickly, standing and pulling back her chair. "Let's get out of here. I want to be alone with you, really alone," he said, his mouth against her ear.

Jill smiled up at him, but she had registered his evasive answer.

He was not being honest with her about his little excursion that afternoon.

Why?

And did it have something to do with the "grocery list" that had fallen out of his pocket that evening?

Jill resolved again to try to get a look at that paper

as Barringer paid the bill and left the tip. They walked out of the dining room and passed the tenor, who saluted Barringer with two fingers as they passed.

"It's freezing out here," Barringer commented as he settled Jill's coat around her shoulders. "I should have sent one of the busboys out to start the car and warm it up."

"Valet parking only on weekends," Jill told him. "But I expect the singer is in full voice then, too."

"We'll skip it," Barringer said, pushing the door open in front of her. "I think we'll be very good at entertaining ourselves, and take-out food has always been my staple."

Jill sat next to him on the seat on the way home, and clung to his arm as they went into the house.

"Let's go up to my room," Jill said, standing on tiptoe to kiss him lingeringly.

"With your father still awake in his study?"

"He won't even realize we're home."

"I don't know, it just seems kind of tacky, like necking on the living room sofa when your parents are in the kitchen."

"Then let's go to your room," she whispered. "He'll never hear us on the third floor." She ran her hand up the inside of his thigh.

He groaned and closed his eyes. "Okay," he said huskily.

They barely made it through the door before falling on the bed. Barringer pulled her sweater over her head with one hand as he yanked off his jacket and tie with the other. Jill unbuckled his belt with hasty fingers and then fumbled with the button on his pants. He dropped his jacket and pushed her hands away, taking off his pants and then easing her back on the bed. He shoved her skirt up to her waist and then stripped off her underclothes, looming above her as she wound her legs around his hips eagerly.

When he entered her they both groaned aloud with the sensation. Jill pressed her face into his shoulder, digging her fingers into his upper arms, covered by the starched cotton of the shirt he still wore. He bore down on her and she surged back up to him, striving in his arms, kissing his lips, his cheek, the hollow of his throat as he carried her with him to a fevered conclusion.

Afterward they lay still, unable to talk, as their breathing calmed down and their runaway heartbeats slowed to normal.

"Wow," Jill finally said. "I never knew it could be like that."

"It can," he replied drowsily. "And it will just get better and better with us."

"Let's take this off," she said, unbuttoning his shirt. "I want to see you."

He allowed her to strip off his shirt, then collapsed on the bed as she began to kiss his body.

"I'm asleep," he said.

Jill ran her tongue down his abdomen, across his thigh, licking him intimately until he put his hand to the back of her neck and held her head against him, his respiration increasing.

"No, you're not," she cooed, stroking him. "Look."

"I've created a monster," he moaned, sitting up and pulling her on top of him.

She sat on his thighs as he closed his eyes and turned his head to the side, his lips parted.

"You learn fast," he said huskily as she took him inside her. He felt bathed in warmth, enclosed and surrounded by it.

"I always was a quick study," she answered.

He let her take the initiative, lying prone as she made love to him. She moving seductively, teasing him until he seized her and wrestled her under him, holding her down on the bed.

"I love you," he said tenderly, looking at her. "Nothing will change that, ever."

"I love you, too," Jill whispered.

He bent his head to kiss her and they took it more slowly this time, enjoying the ride, as he guided her to a gentler conclusion. This time Barringer did fall asleep, and Jill slipped out from under him, donning his shirt to go down one flight and take a shower in her bathroom.

When she emerged she got dressed and went back upstairs to pull a blanket over him and pick his clothes up off the floor. As she was hanging up his suit she saw the jeans he had worn earlier tossed over his desk chair. The paper she was curious about was lying on the floor where it had fallen from his pocket once again.

Jill was tempted, felt guilty for about three seconds, and then snatched the note and unfolded it.

She read it, looked stunned, then read it again.

Then she marched over to the bed and yanked the blanket off Barringer's sleeping form, startling him awake.

"Get up, you...you...liar," she yelled, choking back tears of anger and betrayal. "Get up and start explaining yourself, now!"

Chapter 8

Barringer jumped out of bed stark naked, confused with sleep, his hair in his eyes.

"What the hell are you doing?" he demanded.

Jill whipped out the letter she had found and stuck it under his nose, shaking it.

It took him a moment to register what it was, and then he sighed heavily, slumping into a sitting position on the bed. Every line of his body expressed defeat.

"Why were you reading my mail?" he asked quietly.

"Why was I reading your mail! Is that all you have to say to me?" Jill hissed.

"I don't know what I can say. It's obvious from your demeanor that you think you have everything all figured out, as usual."

"Oh? Am I mistaken about something? Were you or were you not sent here to spy on my father?"

Barringer did not meet her eyes. "Yes."

"Then where is my error? Please, tell me, I am trying to understand."

"That was not the whole assignment."

"Really? And what was the rest of it, pray tell? To pretend to protect us?"

"No pretense."

"So you weren't involved in the adventure of the bloody desk or the dead mouse caper? You didn't set those incidents up in order to make us believe we needed protection?"

Now he did look at her.

"Why are you wearing that indignant expression?" Jill demanded. "Is it so outrageous for me to conclude that you created the problem so you could come in here like a white knight on the proverbial steed to solve it, while in reality you were using that as an excuse to investigate my father?"

"That isn't how it happened." Barringer got up and pulled on his jeans, thumbing his hair back from his forehead distractedly. He tried to take her arm but she yanked it away from him.

"Jill, listen to me. None of that has anything to do with the way I feel about you," he said, trying to maintain the outward appearance of a calm he did not feel.

Jill whirled to face him, her eyes brimming. "How can you say that to me? You have been lying to me from the beginning! You came slithering in here like a snake, getting us to like you and trust you, and the whole damn time you were looking for evidence against my father! Now I understand about the middle-of-the-night computer raid and all the mystery messages and phone calls. What is my father supposed to have done, anyway?''

"Somebody was passing on research secrets to a Middle Eastern contact. The bureau had it narrowed down to a handful of people who were doing that kind of work for them. They must have just found out recently who it was because I got the letter you read clearing your father of suspicion just today.''

"Oh, I see. There was no real evidence that he had done anything wrong, he just happened to fall into the suspect group.''

"Yes.''

"And when you got that letter you knew for sure my father wasn't guilty.''

"Right.''

"Which explains your jovial mood this evening and the sudden desire for a romantic dinner,'' she said sarcastically, wiping her wet cheek with the back of her hand.

"When I got that message I thought you would never have to know,'' he said quietly.

"Know what? That you are the biggest liar God ever created? I think I would have found that out sooner or later.'' She closed her eyes, squeezing out a stream of tears.

"Jill, I was tormented every day I was here. I

wanted to make love to you from the first moment I saw you!''

She made an impatient, disgusted sound.

"Can you imagine what it was like for me," he continued pleadingly, trying to hold her gaze as she turned her head away from him, "wanting you so badly, seeing that you wanted me, too, but all the time knowing that I was—"

"Betraying the trust of someone who was falling in love with you?" she suggested when he stopped talking.

He sighed. "Yes."

She snorted. "I can see how that would be such a terrible burden for your delicate conscience," she replied derisively, shooting him a hostile glance.

"Jill, what could I do?" he demanded of her in agony, spreading his hands.

"You could have told me the truth!"

"And disregard the good faith of the people who had sent me here? If your father *had* been the traitor, and you had alerted him because of what I revealed to you, that would have made me a traitor, too!"

"You should have let me make that decision," Jill said to him coldly. "You should have believed in me enough to know I would do the right thing."

"I'm sorry," he said flatly, his tone unapologetic. "I couldn't take that chance. Not with national security at stake."

"Oh, please, don't give me another speech about taking oaths and handling Bibles, it would sound

very hollow coming from you now," Jill retorted
jeeringly.

He doubled his fists in frustration and banged
them against the wall, causing the articles on his
desk to jump.

"Can't you appreciate the position I was in?" he
demanded, his voice rising. "I wasn't supposed to
get involved with somebody I was guarding in the
first place, that's like the prime directive for an agent
on a protection assignment. You hated me when I
kissed you one moment, then pulled away the
next—my waffling drove you crazy. I am sure you
recall those episodes."

"Oh, I see," Jill said, sniffing. "This is all my
fault now."

He held up his hand to silence her.

"But I went against protocol and allowed that to
happen finally because I simply couldn't resist you
anymore," he added. "I reasoned that I could just
quit the bureau and take my lumps for it once I came
clean with the truth. But the one thing I couldn't tell
you was about the covert investigation of your father. That went way beyond me overstepping my
professional bounds with you or just losing my position. That was treason."

"Oh, please stop," Jill cried, putting her hands
over her ears. "I don't want to hear your rationali-
zations, they mean absolutely nothing to me now."

He fell silent, watching her the way a boxer
watches his opponent, waiting for the next move.

Jill looked at him, her eyes narrowed. "And

knowing all of this, you had the nerve to ask me to marry you."

"After I got that letter I thought you would never know about my investigation of your father, so all I had to do was quit the bureau and we could be together."

She stared at him. "And that makes your previous deception okay? What system of morals are you operating under? Do whatever it takes to get what you want, and as long as you get what you want, everything you did to get it is okay? I believe that is called 'the end justifies the means,' and I have never lived that way. I won't."

"You're not even listening to me, Jill," he said, throwing up his hands.

"Oh, yes I am. I am just replying with something you don't want to hear." Her tears welled up again and she forced them back, swallowing hard. "My father has devoted the last ten years to research that he was turning over to our government in an effort to provide for our defense. You have seen firsthand since you've been here the kind of abuse he has taken for it, the abuse we both have taken. And his government's thanks for that was to send you to spy on him."

Barringer looked at the floor. "I don't choose the assignments or develop the rationale for them," he said quietly.

"You conned me, Tony," she said softly, her pain and anguish almost palpable in her tone. "I thought you came here to protect me, but in reality you only wanted to get the goods on my father. You deceived me, you invaded my privacy, you won my trust and used it against me.''

A silence fell as he made no reply. He couldn't think of the right words to refute her. It had happened basically as she said, but her description made it sound so clinical and brutal, so unfeeling.

He had really never planned to break her heart.

Jill watched him, waiting hopelessly for him to defend himself, waiting for him to tell her that she was mistaken, deceived, unaware of some new information that would absolve him of all wrongdoing and make everything okay between them. But she knew that was not going to happen. First Brian, now Tony—she could not seem to find a man who would be honest with her. Why was she such an idiot? Once again she had chosen a liar and a betrayer.

And the worst of it was she was still in love with him.

He raised his eyes to hers. ''And now you can't forgive me,'' he said dully, hopelessly. He was leaning against the wall, his muscular arms folded, clad only in his jeans, his feet and torso bare. His dark hair, untidy from sleep, curled around his ears and down the sides of his neck. Even knowing what he had done, her reaction to him was so visceral and so intense that she had never wanted him more than she did at that moment.

This knowledge of her own weakness infuriated her.

''Get out,'' she said to him.

He stared at her.

"You heard me."

"Look, Jill, I know you are angry with me now…"

"Angry?" She tore the engagement ring off her finger and threw it at him. It bounced off his arm and landed on the floor, where it rolled under his desk.

He looked at it, then back at Jill.

She picked up his shirt and tossed it at his head. He caught it deftly with one hand.

"You'd better put it on, it's pretty cold outside," Jill advised him, licking the tears from her lips as she spoke. "Oh, and you'll need this, too," she added, grabbing his down jacket from the chair and throwing it at his feet.

He was still rooted to the floor, watching her.

"Get out!" she screamed at the top of her lungs. "Get out, get out, get out!" She rushed at him, beating at his chest. At first he tried to hold her and calm her down, but when he saw that it was impossible he released her, stepping back from her and picking up his coat as she continued to rain blows on him. He dodged them as best he could and went into the hall, where Jill, crying hysterically, watched him stumble down the steps to the landing. She ran back into his room and grabbed his shoes, following him down the stairs until she caught up with him outside her father's office.

"And don't forget these!" she shrieked after him, firing one of the leather Top-Siders at his head.

He dodged the missile and stopped to put it on when it fell beside him, then straightened and caught the other shoe as it came sailing toward him.

"I'll be back to talk to you when you're a little more rational, Jill," he said evenly, stepping into the second shoe and pulling his coat onto his arms. "I'll tell your father's guard outside to take over for you and your father until my replacement arrives."

Jill yelled with frustration and grabbed a plant sitting on a stand to her left. She heaved the heavy china pot at his head and it exploded against the closing front door as Barringer went through it. Greenery and potting soil cascaded to the hardwood floor in a shower of murky water and painted porcelain shards.

"What on earth is going on out here?" Arthur Darcy demanded crossly, emerging from his office to find his daughter on the verge of collapse, in floods of tears.

"Oh, Daddy," Jill sobbed, "it's all too awful." She threw herself into her father's arms and Arthur patted her on the back awkwardly as she cried.

"There, there," Arthur said, glancing at the front hall, where his potted ivy lay in a puddled mess, its roots exposed, its tendrils spread out on the floor awkwardly. He led her into the kitchen and sat her in a chair, then put the kettle on for tea. He pulled out a chair and sat across from his daughter, taking her hand as she sniffled, wiping her eyes with the hem of her shirt.

"Now, tell me all about it," he said.

Jill took a sobbing breath, nodded and began to relate the unhappy tale.

Barringer walked into downtown Longmeadow, which was closed up for the night, with the wind whistling around his bare ankles and freezing his fingers, which he kept jammed in his coat pockets. He used the pay phone at the twenty-four-hour diner to call a cab and got a cup of coffee to go. He stood sipping it inside the glass-walled entrance as he waited for the taxi. Thank God his wallet had been in his jeans or he would have been on the street without money or ID.

He refused to panic. While this was probably the lowest he had ever felt in his life, he knew from experience that people always calmed down after the initial shock of any bad news. Jill had every right to be angry, but she couldn't sustain the level of fury he had just seen forever. When she settled down she would think about things and give him another chance.

It was all his fault, she was right. He had behaved like an idiot. If he had not been so hot to get her into bed earlier that night he would not have brought her to his room. She would not have found that letter. And she never would have known about his investigation of her father. He'd known it was a risk to have her up there, he'd known he had documents in there he did not want her to see, but all he could think about at the time was making love to her.

And this debacle was the result.

He looked up as the taxi pulled to the curb in front of the diner. He went out and told the driver to take him to the Springfield airport. He could catch the shuttle from there to Washington.

As he settled into the back seat of the cab he thought about what he had to do: arrange new protection for Jill, come clean with the bureau, then resign his position.

Then he had to get Jill back.

Some things were a lot easier to accomplish than others.

Arthur Darcy regarded his daughter gravely. He looked like he had aged ten years during the time she had been talking.

"Are you absolutely sure about all of this, Jill?" he asked, his voice low and tired.

Jill nodded. She was aware of how her father must be feeling about the suspicion that had been focused on him, but she was so immersed in her own pain she didn't know how to console him.

"Tony was here to investigate me as well as protect you? He had two assignments, as it were?"

"Yes. I just found out about his hidden agenda today, that's why I threw him out tonight." She snatched a tissue from the box on the table and blew her nose.

"And what did he say?"

"Oh, what was he going to say? He was just doing his job, it was a matter of national security, he's as innocent as a lamb." She crumpled the tissue in her palm. "You know, I saw things that made me suspicious, made me wonder, but when he dismissed them I believed him. I wanted to believe him."

Arthur stood up and patted her shoulder. "It's late, Jill. We should both go to bed. I have some calls to make in the morning and you...well...you have to start the process of getting over this."

"I don't think I can," she whispered, and put her hand to her mouth to stifle a sob.

"Yes, you can," her father said firmly. "If I can get over the fact that the people I have been working for during the last decade can sic a spy on me, then you can forget Antony Barringer." He regarded her measuringly. "It may be bad timing but I have to say this." Arthur sighed. "I don't know that you should try."

Jill stared at him. "What do you mean?"

"I think Tony was caught in an impossible situation. He came here with a job to do, he didn't know he would fall in love with you. You shouldn't take Tony's mission personally, Jill. I don't. I realize that's easy for me to say because I am not in love with him, but from what you just told me he was and is willing to sacrifice his job, his career, to be with you. What further proof do you need that he does love you? It may have begun badly or for the wrong reasons, but I think he has proved his good intentions with his proposal and his plans for your shared future."

Jill was silent.

"Will you consider what I've said?" her father inquired.

Jill nodded.

"Good night, my dear."

Jill watched her father walk toward the hall slowly, as if the information she had just given him had impaired his usual brisk step.

"What are you going to do, Dad?" she called after him.

"I am going to check on this in the morning, and if what you say is true, and I don't doubt that it is, I will terminate my relationship with the federal government immediately. I won't take another dime of their money and I won't do another minute's research for them."

Jill was proud of the quiet conviction in his voice.

"Don't sell Tony short," Arthur added as he left. "Think about it."

Jill heard him going up the stairs to his bedroom.

She put her head down on her folded arms and considered what her father had said. He was in a position to be more detached and reasonable than she could ever be. Her mind was so clouded by her turbulent feelings that objectivity was not even an option.

All she knew was how much it hurt when she thought about Tony deceiving her. In a perfect universe she might be able to see the whole episode in balance, the way her father did, but she was a woman in love. The whole world might be able to forgive Tony, but she was having a tough time with it.

Nevertheless, her father's words haunted her.

Was he right?

Things happened pretty quickly during the next couple of weeks. Arthur Darcy dropped his research project in outrage and called a press conference ten days after Barringer's departure. Darcy announced that he had been signed by a private foundation in Boston that had been pursuing him for years. He refused to give a reason for abandoning his government grant but made it clear that he would no longer be doing weapons-related work.

The pacifists on campus claimed victory, assuming that Arthur had finally seen the light—or been driven to the decision by their harassment—and their protests ceased.

Jill was happy that the whole episode was over, and even happier that she would not have to deal with another FBI operative, since the feds no longer had a reason to guard her father and the danger had passed. She should have felt better about the end of a bad period in her life, but the memories of her time with Antony Barringer haunted her, robbing her of rest, motivation, peace. She went through the motions of attending classes and teaching like a sleepwalker, always missing the one person who had been with her while she did these things, and hating herself intensely for missing him.

She told herself she was better off without him,

but it didn't feel that way. Her father's words lingered: Arthur Darcy was an intelligent man and he
didn't blame Tony. Should she? But then, it didn't
matter even if Arthur was right. Tony was gone. She
was still in love with him, maybe she always would
be, but the bridges were burned.

It was over.

Michelle came to the Darcy house for lunch the
day after Arthur's announcement, which was carried
in all the newspapers and mentioned on the local
television news. Carrie, who had been hovering
around Jill since she heard about Barringer's departure, offered to make the meal. The two young
women sat in the kitchen sipping sodas while Carrie
moved in the background, ladling soup into bowls.

They all looked up as the doorbell rang.

"I'll get it," Carrie said, and they heard Carrie
answering the door. A minute later she came into
the kitchen carrying a box wrapped in brown paper.

"For you," Carrie said, handing Jill the package.

Jill examined the return address, which was just
a phone number from a courier office in Boston, and
then ripped off the wrapping.

Inside was a shoe box, and the sight gave her a
chill.

"What is it?" Carrie asked.

"That dead mouse came in a shoe box," Jill murmured.

"But that's over," Michelle said. "Your father
isn't doing that work anymore."

"Right."

"So there's nothing to protest."

"Maybe you shouldn't open it," Carrie said worriedly. "You can't tell who it is from and it could be anything."

"Oh, well, it isn't ticking," Jill said, and lifted the cover.

Inside was a dead squirrel with a sign taped to it.

"You're next," it read.

Chapter 9

Michelle glanced at the note and then looked away.

"I'm calling the police," Carrie said, and went to the phone.

Jill dropped the lid of the shoe box with a shaking hand.

"I can't believe this," she whispered. "Why? The peace people got what they wanted. My father dropped the research, he told the world about it. Why are they still sending this stuff?"

"Maybe they didn't send it," Michelle said.

Jill looked at her fearfully. "What do you mean?"

"Maybe they never sent any of it. Maybe there's somebody else behind it."

"Michelle, the peace movement took credit for the blood on my desk at the school."

Michelle looked thoughtful. "Yes," she said. "I had forgotten about that."

"Then why is this stuff still coming?" Jill asked, gesturing disgustedly to the box.

"Splinter group?" Michelle suggested. "One of the crazies who's just a little crazier than the others and who doesn't think your father has been punished enough?"

"It was addressed to me."

"That's still the best way to upset your father."

"I don't know." Jill sighed. "You'd think they'd play nice by now. From their point of view they got exactly what they wanted. They don't know that my father gave up his research for his own reasons, they think he did it to placate them. There is simply no reason for this to continue any longer."

Michelle patted Jill's shoulder. "Look, take it easy. The package was sent by a commercial carrier. The police will be able to track it, right down to which employee received it in the first place and who delivered it here."

"It originated at that huge depot in Boston, Michelle. The place must handle thousands of packages a day, long lines, bored employees dealing with anonymous customers."

"Maybe they have video cameras taping the customers," Michelle suggested.

Jill shrugged. She considered it a long shot. She

was also sure that the name and telephone number listed on the UPS duplicate slip would be phonies.

Would this never end? And the idea that now she had to face the prospect of more such surprises without the comfort and strength of Tony's support terrified her.

The police arrived and took the usual statements and did the usual sniffing around the house. It was clear to Jill that they didn't understand why she had gotten another delivery as they had considered the case closed. Her father was called back from Boston and Carrie tried to insist on staying until he arrived. Michelle convinced the older woman that they would be fine in the house with the police guard out front. By the time everyone left Jill felt like an exposed nerve.

It wasn't over, the threat was still there, and now Tony was not with her to protect her.

She was afraid.

Barringer replaced the receiver of the phone in his hotel room in Springfield and lay down on the hard bed with its striped spread, staring at the flocked wallpaper.

The phone call had been from Carrie. He had given her his number, calling her when he knew Jill would be at school. She had told him about the latest delivery at the Darcy house and had left the next move to him. And that move was simple: Jill was still in danger, so he had to act. Now.

For the first time he allowed himself to think that

maybe he would not get Jill back, that maybe it *was* over, that she would not recover from the wound he had inflicted and that she would never let him back into her life. It was like contemplating the reality of death. He closed his eyes and rolled over, fully dressed, forcing his mind to go in another direction. Somebody was still stalking Jill, and that issue was separate and apart from his possible future with her.

He had no intention of going away and leaving her alone as long as she was in danger.

He got up and grabbed a notebook and pencil from the hotel desk. He made notes about everybody and everything he had experienced with Jill since the first day of his assignment with her. He worked into the evening and fell asleep on the bed, then got up in the morning and ordered room service coffee. He came out of the shower as it arrived, and he was pouring the first cup when it hit him. The knowledge burst upon him so suddenly he almost scalded himself with the hot brew, and he put the cup down carefully, his heart racing.

Craig. Joe Craig, the guy who had been mauling Jill when he first arrived to guard her. Craig, who lost the fight to him and then seemed to back down, accepting his transfer from Jill's class to Michelle's without objection. But maybe, just maybe, he had gone underground, channeling his resentment of Jill's rejection into a long-term plan to terrorize her, using the protest of the pacifists as a cover.

The more Barringer thought about it, the more sense it made, and he dressed on the run, grabbing

his revolver and stuffing it inside his jacket. He had
returned his bureau-issued firearms but he still had
a permit to carry a gun as a private citizen, and as
he ran down to his car he thought about Craig. Michelle and Jill had said he was a weapons obsessive
with military experience. Barringer grabbed a box
of bullets from his glove compartment and crammed
it into his jeans pocket.

He broke all speed limits getting to the college.
He knew Jill's schedule and she was in a lecture
that her TA students shared with Michelle's class on
the top floor of the literature building. Craig should
be there, too. He had to get Jill away from the class,
and then he would send the police after Craig. He
was so sure he was right that he didn't worry about
causing a ruckus for no reason or alarming people
unnecessarily. It would take forever to convince the
police that Craig was the culprit, then convince a
prosecutor to ask a judge to issue a warrant. They
would want to do all the preliminaries by the book,
which would eat time. So he had to act alone. Every
second Jill was with Craig she was in danger, the
guy could explode at any moment. The only thing
that puzzled Barringer was why it had taken him so
long to realize what was going on. His emotional
involvement with Jill must have clouded his judgment. He had accepted the common opinion that the
peace group on campus was responsible for all the
incidents, when he should have known that the last
two "gifts" were different, more personal, more
menacing. They weren't sent by somebody who

wanted to make a political point. They were sent by somebody harboring a grudge who wanted to intimidate and upset the recipient.

And if he hadn't spent the last month in a haze of romance-induced stupidity he would have seen what was right under his nose.

He went up the stairs two at a time, and then halted in the lobby outside the lecture hall. He was wondering how he could get a glimpse inside without being seen when Michelle came out of the double doors and walked toward him.

He snaked his arm out to grab her. She gasped and started to struggle, then relaxed when she saw his face.

"Tony! What are you doing here?" she demanded.

"Where's Jill?" he demanded.

"She's inside, but she's not going to talk to you," Michelle replied. "Please don't make a scene here...."

"Is Joe Craig in there with her?" Barringer asked.

"Well, yes, he's in the combined lecture."

"Michelle, listen to me," Barringer said, taking her aside and lowering his voice. "Craig is the one who's been sending Jill those packages and I think he is dangerous. I have to get her out of there and away from him, and then I want you to call the police and explain the situation. Ask for Lieutenant Blackman and say I told you to call."

"Joe Craig?" Michelle whispered, her eyes wide.

"Yes. Now, as soon as I get Jill out of there, you do exactly as I told you..."

They both looked up as the auditorium doors opened and the students poured out, Joe Craig a few steps behind Jill. Craig saw Barringer first and understood why he had returned in an instant. Craig dodged forward and grabbed Jill, putting one arm across her throat from behind and pulling a pistol from his jacket pocket with his other hand. Jill was too stunned to make a sound, but when she saw Barringer standing across the lobby she knew why he was there.

"Back off," Craig yelled to Barringer, as several onlookers screamed when they saw Craig's gun. "If you come after me she gets it." He dragged Jill, who beseeched Barringer with her eyes, across the hall as everyone froze like statues before them. He ducked into the back stairwell with Jill in tow.

"Call the police!" Barringer barked over his shoulder to Michelle as he dashed after them.

He ran down the stairs, catching up to them on the landing as Craig's progress was slowed by Jill's struggles. Barringer pulled out his pistol and rested one wrist on top of the other, squinting to get a safe shot at Craig that would keep Jill in the clear. Jill was at arm's length from Craig as he tried to force her down the steps and Barringer saw his opportunity. He aimed and fired once, hitting Craig in the leg to stop him but not kill him. Jill screamed as the pistol report echoed around the stairwell and Craig released her as he fell.

"Jill, come to me!" Barringer called, and she scrambled to her feet, sobbing as she leapt up the steps to reach Barringer. Just as she reached him and his arm came out to embrace her Craig rolled over and half sat, grabbing his injured leg with one hand and aiming his gun with the other. Barringer saw him moving and shoved Jill aside. She hit the wall behind him as another shot rang out and Barringer collapsed, gasping, clutching his chest.

"Tony!" she screamed, horrified as a scarlet flower blossomed on his shirt and his gun fell from his hand. He slipped to the floor as she glanced down at Craig and saw that he was prone, his eyes closed, incapable of further action.

Jill knelt beside Barringer and cradled his head in her lap.

"You're going to be fine," she told him, taking off her sweater and staunching the flow of his blood with it, stroking his cheek. His eyes were open but his lids were fluttering, his gaze unfocused. She spread her coat over his legs.

"You…okay?" he muttered, trying to sit up.

"Yes, yes, I'm fine. Tony, please stay quiet," she pleaded, as the door at the top of the stairwell opened just a crack and a student's white, frightened face appeared.

"Call an ambulance!" Jill yelled. "There's been a shooting! I have an injured man here."

The door slammed shut and Jill heard running footsteps.

"Where…Craig?" Barringer rasped, craning his neck to try to look around him.

"He's unconscious, Tony. Oh, please lie still," Jill sobbed, aware that he probably had a cell phone on his person but afraid to move him to look for it.

"He's the one… I just realized it. He's the one…sending…dead animals."

"Yes, yes. Don't talk." She wrapped the sweater more tightly against his body and moaned helplessly when she saw the amount of blood he was losing.

"Dangerous…" he whispered, sweat breaking out on his face, his voice fading. "They kill animals, then they…kill…people…." His eyes closed slowly.

The door opened again and a voice called down to her. "Ambulance on the way!"

"Oh, thank God. Did you hear that, Tony? You're going to be okay, the ambulance is coming." She bent over him and his lashes lifted. His green eyes were cloudy.

"I love you," he murmured.

"I love you, too, Tony. I'm so sorry," Jill sobbed, kissing him on the lips. "I was coming to find you, I decided it last night. I was just going to finish out the day and then call you. Carrie said you were nearby, she said you had called and given her your new number…."

She stopped talking. His eyes were closed again.

She snatched his hand and held it to her mouth, trying to warm it. "I will make it all up to you, I promise,'' she babbled. ''You'll get well, and we'll start over, just as you wanted.''

The stairwell echoed with her terrified words and she fell silent again. She had to do something, but what? She could not leave Tony alone but she had to save his life. She had never felt more helpless, and never more aware of how very much she loved the man who lay bleeding in her arms.

The thought that Tony might die made all her past considerations of pride and hurt feelings fade into obscurity.

Nothing mattered now except saving Tony's life.

The door opened again and Michelle appeared. When she saw the carnage below on the stairs she covered her mouth with both hands, her eyes enormous.

''Lord help us,'' she whispered.

''Michelle, will you take the gun away from Craig? I'm afraid he's going to wake up again and use it. I can't leave Tony.''

''I can't touch it,'' Michelle gasped. ''I called the police. Let them handle it when they get here.''

''Michelle, you have to do it! Everybody else is afraid to come down here and he could regain consciousness at any time. Tony just shot him in the leg, he's not badly hurt.''

Michelle closed her eyes briefly, as if in prayer, then began to pick her way down the stairs, pausing momentarily to look down at Tony semiconscious in Jill's lap, a pool of blood spreading beneath him. She moved on down to the landing and stopped a

                                     Made for Each Other

short distance from Joe Craig, who lay sprawled bonelessly on the cement, his gun two feet away from his hand.

"Do it!" Jill urged her. "Use your scarf."

Michelle pulled the scarf from her neck and bent to pick up the gun from the floor, handling it with two fingers, gingerly.

"Good," Jill said, sighing. "Bring it up here."

As Michelle was ascending the staircase they heard sirens wailing in the distance, coming closer.

"The police," Michelle said gratefully.

"I hope to God it's the ambulance," Jill replied. She looked down at Barringer and saw that he was unconscious now, his breathing shallow, his color very pale. His shirt was soaked with blood and his hands were clammy.

"Hang on, darling," Jill whispered, bending to talk into his ear even though he probably could not hear what she was saying. "Help is on the way."

They waited for what seemed like hours until suddenly the doors burst open from above and two policemen arrived, while two more came running up from below, guns drawn. When they took in the scene they holstered their guns. Jill tried to tell them what had happened as minutes later the paramedics showed up, too. The small hallway was suddenly jammed with bodies in uniforms and loud with the sound of terse commands from the medical personnel. When Barringer was lifted from her lap and loaded onto a stretcher Jill tried to run after him and was restrained by one of the cops.

"Please let me go," Jill begged. "I can ride with him in the ambulance."

A paramedic took pity on her and nodded to the cop, who released Jill.

"Michelle, will you stay here and tell them anything else they need to know?" Jill called back to her friend. "I'll be at the hospital with Tony."

Michelle nodded dumbly, her expression still stunned, as if she were unable to absorb what had just happened.

Jill ran after the stretcher as the medics carried it down the stairs and out the doors to the waiting ambulance. She jumped up behind it and went inside, sitting on a shelf across from Barringer as the medics knelt on either side of him and began taking readings.

"Are you the next of kin?" one of them asked her.

"I guess so," she replied. "I don't think he has anybody else. Maybe a cousin." She started to cry.

"Do you know his blood type?"

"I…think there should be an ID card in his wallet, back pocket," Jill replied.

The medic searched and produced the card. "Type O, certified HIV negative as of three months ago, federal medical ID 348960," he said to his colleague, who nodded and opened a foam container.

"BP is ninety over fifty-five," one of the others said, and Jill closed her eyes despairingly.

She knew that was really low.

"Is he going to make it?" she asked the one who seemed to be in charge.

"We're doing everything we can for him, miss," the medic replied evenly.

It was the standard answer, and it told her nothing.

The rest of the ambulance ride was a blur that she would relive in her nightmares for years to come. She watched them hanging plastic bags of blood and various other solutions that ran through tubes and into Barringer's veins as they roared through the midmorning traffic to the hospital, siren blaring. She held Tony's cold hand and told him that he would be okay, that she loved him, and that all of this would be over soon. The medical exchanges formed a droning background to her one-way conversation. When they arrived at the emergency room the back doors of the ambulance opened and the medics jumped out, whisking Barringer away as she followed more slowly. Just as she went inside another ambulance pulled up and she saw Craig being transported past her.

I'll make sure you pay, sucker, Jill thought, wondering if she had ever hated another human being this much.

The plastic chairs in the ER waiting room seemed like furniture in a second home to her. Since she met Barringer she had spent more time in this place than she had in the library at school.

She slumped into a seat and looked down at her clothes, which were covered with Barringer's blood.

So much, she thought. So much blood. How could he possibly survive the loss of it?

Hours went by, and every time she asked at the desk she was told that Barringer was still in surgery. Michelle arrived to keep her company and they had sat in silence for another interval before a weary young surgeon in green scrubs came into the room and called out, "Anybody here for Antony Barringer?"

Jill jumped up and ran to him anxiously.

"He's alive, barely," the surgeon said in a tired voice, untying his mask. The name tag on his breast read "Gilroy, Thomas. M.D."

Jill nodded, afraid to speak.

"The bullet just missed his heart, nicked the aorta, went on a downward trajectory and nicked the spleen. We removed it, but he has lost a lot of blood. We ran a series of tests to see if there were any other internal injuries and we couldn't find any. So it boils down to this—if he can recover from the shock and the blood loss he'll be fine. On the positive side, most people who have lost as much blood as he did would be dead already, exsanguinated. And he is young and fit and strong, factors that should never be discounted."

Jill cleared her throat. "At this point you have no idea what will happen?" she managed to say.

"No. He could arrest at any time, he could throw a clot or start bleeding again from an injury we could not find. Or his blood pressure could climb back to normal and he could be out of the hospital next week. I have seen cases like this go either way. They're critical for a day or so and then they either die or get better quickly.''

''I see,'' she whispered.

He put his hand on her shoulder comfortingly.

''Hang in there,'' he said. ''He's in great physical condition. And if I were in his place and had you waiting for me I would certainly come back to you.''

Jill nodded again, trying to smile, her eyes flooding. He was kind. ''Can I see him?''

''I'm sorry, no. He's in intensive care and the next twelve hours will be critical to his recovery. If he improves overnight maybe you can see him tomorrow.''

''What room is he in?''

''Check at the desk,'' he said, and turned away, walking back inside the treatment room. He had done his work with Barringer and his mind was already moving on to his next case.

Jill looked around to find Michelle standing behind her.

''Did you hear what the doctor said?'' Jill asked.

''Yes.''

''He has to live,'' Jill sobbed. ''I know he will. I will spend my life with him and have his children and grow old with him. He has to live.''

''Of course he will live.'' Michelle took her hands and led her back to their seats.

''Why did it take so long for me to see what was really important?'' She shook her head. ''He's at death's door now because he was worried about me.

Even after how badly I had treated him, he came back.''

"He loves you. He figured out that it was Joe Craig behind those packages. He was trying to get you out of the lecture hall before Joe saw him.''

Jill reached for her hand and squeezed it. "Oh, Michelle, how could you watch me being such a fool? How must all of this look to you?''

"It looks like two people who fell in love under bad circumstances,'' Michelle said, echoing Jill's father. "You're my friend and Tony is a stand-up guy who has helped me more than once. There are no villains in this story.'' Michelle stood and said, "Now, why don't we go to your house so you can take a shower and change those clothes?''

"I don't want to leave Tony.''

"Jill, you heard the doctor,'' Michelle said gently. "Tony is in intensive care, you won't be able to see him until tomorrow. You sitting here in these filthy clothes won't do anybody any good. I'll go over to the clerk and find out what room Tony will be in and leave your name and number to be contacted about any changes in his condition. I'll be right back, okay?''

Jill nodded, too worn out to raise any further objections.

Michelle walked away and Jill stared at the pattern in the green-and-black tiled floor. When Michelle returned Jill got up and followed her out to Michelle's car.

Chapter 10

Barringer was tied down in a bed, unable to move, and there was a three-hundred-pound gorilla on his chest. It hurt to breathe, there was something stuck down his throat and up his nose, and he had to go to the bathroom.

Where the hell was he?

He tried to open his eyes and nothing happened. He tried again and was rewarded with a blurred view of a white ceiling. He looked sideways and saw bulky instruments at his side, then looked the other way and saw several bags hanging above his head. His hands were tied with gauze to the sidebars of a bed.

He was in a hospital.

As soon as that realization dawned he remembered what had happened. He tried to sit up and couldn't move.

He tried to say Jill's name and croaked instead.

A nurse appeared from beyond his field of vision and her face swam above him.

"He's coming out of it," she said to somebody Barringer couldn't see. "Welcome back," she added to Barringer, and smiled.

He tugged on his left hand and she quickly untied it.

"Sorry about that," she said. "You kept trying to pull your ventilator out during your sleep."

He pointed to the plastic tube in his mouth.

She glanced at the machine at his side and said, "Your pulse ox is fine, I guess that can come out." She removed the ventilator and he licked his lips. She pulled the nose clip out and released the band from the back of his head.

"Find Dr. Gilroy on rounds and tell him his patient in room 318 is waking up," the nurse said, and a figure detached itself from the side of the bed and went out of the room.

"Jill?" Barringer said again, louder this time.

"If Jill is the young woman who has been waiting out in the hall for the last six hours, I am sure she will be in as soon as Dr. Gilroy says you can have a visitor."

"She okay?"

"She looks fine to me," the nurse said brightly.

He closed his eyes, relieved. After a few seconds his lashes lifted again and he said, "Drink?"

The nurse produced a carafe from his bedside table and poured him a glass of water. "Drink all you want. We're trying to replenish your blood supply. That's what all this is about." She gestured to the bags of blood, saline and glucose solution hanging on a metal stand next to his bed. She put a straw in the glass and he drained it, gasping for breath when he was done.

"Take it easy," she said, smiling. "You cruised the pearly gates yesterday and you're not out of the woods yet."

"Bathroom?" he said.

"You're just feeling the pressure from the catheter. Don't worry about it, that should come out soon, too."

He tried to move his right side and groaned deeply.

"That's where you took the bullet, sweetie," she said, patting his hand. "It's going to hurt like the dickens for a while. Just twist this little ring on the tube here if you want more pain meds. You can have as much as you want for the next couple of days."

Barringer didn't touch it. He didn't want to be dopey if Jill came to see him.

His door opened and a man in a white coat walked in and stood at his side.

"Hi, Tony, I'm Dr. Gilroy. I performed the surgery on you yesterday."

Barringer lifted his hand and the doctor reached across him to shake it firmly.

"You're a very lucky fellow," Gilroy said.

Barringer rolled his eyes.

Gilroy laughed. "You may not feel that way now, but you came close to checking out permanently. I am in a position to tell you that not many who come into the hospital in your condition survive."

Barringer nodded wearily.

"How are you feeling?" the doctor asked.

Barringer tried to shrug, winced and gave up the attempt.

The doctor smiled.

"Jill visit?" Barringer said.

"She's right outside. She'll come in after you've rested, maybe in a couple of hours. One at a time for you for a few days. Anything you want to know before I leave?"

"Craig?" Barringer asked.

Gilroy looked at the nurse, who said in a low tone, "The guy who shot him."

Gilroy nodded thoughtfully.

"Tony, Mr. Craig is under guard in another ward. He'll be released into police custody later today. His injuries were much less severe than yours."

"Wasn't…trying…to kill him."

"Well, he was trying to kill you, and he almost succeeded. But I wouldn't worry about him anymore. He has a long series of charges to face, including attempted murder and assorted weapons and assault felonies. I doubt he'll be seeing the street for years to come. I have a couple of detectives who want to talk to you about all that, but I think the interview can wait for a few days."

"Jill," Barringer said again.

Gilroy grinned. "You're making me feel unwanted, Tony. Now, go back to sleep. She'll be the first person you see when you wake again, I promise."

Barringer's eyes closed.

"He didn't need much persuading," Gilroy said to the nurse. "Watch him, and if he stays stable let the girlfriend come in for a few minutes at around four."

The nurse nodded.

"Don't let her stay too long. Ten minutes tops. I don't want him getting agitated."

"Yes, Doctor."

Jill leapt to her feet in the ward's small lounge as the doctor emerged from Barringer's private room.

"Can I see him?" she demanded, rushing up to Gilroy.

"In good time. Give it another two hours."

"Is he all right?"

"Yes, he's doing very well considering his injuries, but I don't want you tiring him out."

"It's better for him if I stay away?" Jill asked anxiously.

Gilroy nodded. "For the moment."

"All right. Whatever will help. I'll be right here waiting when you give the word."

He smiled and cocked his head at her. "You would do well to go out for a leisurely lunch and then come back to see him."

"I'll stay," Jill said, afraid that if she left there

would be some crisis with Tony. She went back into the lounge to sit with Carrie.

"No luck, huh?" Carrie said.

"He told me to go to lunch."

"That's not a bad idea."

"I don't want lunch. I want to see Tony."

"Jill, you wear me out," Carrie said.

Jill didn't answer, just focused her gaze on the clock at the other end of the room. The hands crawled around it at glacial speed as Carrie rose and got a sandwich from a courtesy cart operated by a volunteer and then sat next to Jill and ate it.

Jill got up at the same moment an aide stuck her head into the lounge and said, "Miss Darcy? You can see Mr. Barringer for a few minutes now."

Jill rushed to follow her as Carrie trailed the duo more slowly, waiting in the hall as Jill entered Barringer's room.

Jill was prepared for him to look bad. She steeled herself for the sight of the heavy growth of beard stubble, the red-rimmed eyes, the forest of tubes and bags, the large, stained dressing that covered one half of his chest. His gaze followed her as she entered, and she stood by the railing on one side of his bed, next to a digital machine that monitored his blood-pressure reading automatically, blipping and flashing numbers every thirty seconds.

"Hi," she said, taking his hand, unable to get another word past the tightness in her throat.

He winked at her. His hair was a mess, matted and standing up against the pillow behind his head, and his muscular arms looked out of place framed by the white sheets of a sickbed.

"You look fine," she said bravely. She had promised herself she was not going to cry.

"Liar," he said hoarsely, and smiled.

"Oh, Tony, I don't know what to say," she whispered, aware of the two nurses standing in the room behind her.

"Don't have to…say anything," he replied.

"When you get out of here you're coming home with me," she said, squeezing his fingers.

He closed his eyes. "Taking charge?" he said softly.

"You bet I am. You've done enough."

"Have to get…job. Pay the bills here. No insurance."

"Don't worry about that, it's all taken care of," Jill said.

His eyes opened and flew to her face. "You didn't…"

"No, I didn't. The feds are picking up the tab. Some bigwig placed a call to Dr. Gilroy and said that you were to have the best care available and Uncle Sam would pay for it. Sounds to me like somebody down in Washington is having an attack of the guilts for calling off the guard too soon and leaving you as a sitting duck."

He shook his head slowly, whether in disbelief or wonder she wasn't sure.

"They also indicated obliquely to Gilroy that you could have your old job back."

Barringer looked at her, then started to laugh, then coughed.

"I think that's enough, Miss Darcy," one of the nurses said behind her.

"Oh, please, just a moment longer," Jill begged, and then stared as Nurse Judy Campbell from the ER appeared in the doorway. She looked at Barringer in the bed and then at Jill.

"I saw Tony's name on the patient roster," she said breathily, her eyes wide.

Tony lifted his hand at her from the bed.

"No more visitors, Judy," Tony's nurse said.

They looked at each other.

"I think it's time we all left," the nurse insisted, gesturing to the door.

"I'll be back in the morning," Jill said to Barringer, and kissed his hand.

"Don't waste 'em, sweetheart," Barringer mumbled.

Jill bent over the bed and kissed him on the mouth as they all watched her.

Judy left on silent shoes.

"Who was that?" Carrie asked as she and Jill walked out of the hospital room together.

"One very disappointed lady," Jill said with satisfaction.

Carrie shrugged. "All right, I am going to feed you before you take up your vigil again. Let's go."

They strolled off down the hall, arm in arm.

Barringer was discharged ten days later, and Jill took him home in a taxi. Carrie had prepared his room and left food in the refrigerator and then discreetly disappeared.

"Awfully quiet here," he commented as they entered the house. "Hospitals are noisy."

"Just you and me," Jill replied, squeezing his arm as he walked with her support.

"Sounds good." He looked at the pile of envelopes on the entry hall table and said, "What's all that mail?"

"I assume they are job inquiries for you. Once your story hit the papers there was no shortage of interest. Not to mention the bureau with egg on its face coming hat in hand to offer you another 'career opportunity.'"

"I did violate the rules, Jill. It's not like I didn't understand the situation."

She took their coats and scarves and hung them on the coatrack in the hall.

"Oh, let's not talk about the past. That's why you had no TV or papers or magazines in the hospital. Gilroy wanted you to forget all that and concentrate on your recovery."

They paused at the foot of the stairs and looked up at them apprehensively.

"Do you want to sit down in the living room first?" Jill asked him worriedly.

"No. I want to take a shower. There was no water pressure on the third floor in the hospital and the shower there was like somebody spitting on my head. Not to mention the dressings and ports I had to keep dry.''

They took the stairs one at a time, slowly, and stopped outside the bathroom across the hall from Jill's room.

''I'll be fine from here,'' he said, and went inside, leaning heavily on the sink. Jill moved behind him to turn on the shower.

''Just go and wait for me in your room,'' he said.

''I'll help you off with your shirt,'' she said, unbuttoning it and pulling the sleeves off his arms. He still had a small dressing over the entry wound on his chest and his jeans hung low on his hips.

He had lost weight.

''Will you go away?'' he said, exasperated. ''You're making me feel like an invalid.''

''You are an invalid. I'm afraid you'll fall.''

''Then come in the shower with me. You can hold me up if you want, but I can't stand this hovering around like I'm about to crash to the floor any minute.''

Jill stripped in ten seconds and then helped him out of the rest of his clothes. They stood together under the stream of water while Barringer soaped his body thoroughly and washed his hair with Jill's arms around his waist. He rinsed luxuriously and then turned to face her, bending to embrace her and lifting her tight against him.

''Tony, no,'' Jill said, pushing back against his shoulders with her hands, careful to avoid his wound. ''You're still weak.''

"I'm never that weak," he said, smiling, and backed her against the wall.

Jill closed her eyes as he nuzzled her neck. She knew she should object again, but she had missed him so much.

"At least let's go into the bedroom," she said weakly. "I don't want us to slip and get killed in here."

He led her by the hand, both of them dripping, to her bed and then lay down on it, wincing. When she drew back at his expression he tugged her forward, toppling her onto him.

"Do you know what I thought about the whole time I was in the hospital?" he said softly, reaching up to pull her head down to him and kiss her.

"Us getting married? That's what you told me."

"Besides that."

"I can't guess. You'll have to show me."

And so he did.

Epilogue

"And this," Barringer said as he opened the door with a flourish, "is what is laughingly known as my apartment."

Jill looked around the large studio curiously. The main room had a dining area at one end of it with a galley kitchen behind a swinging door, and a second room off a short hall contained a bedroom suite and a wall of bookshelves. There were no photographs or items that revealed his personality on the walls or surfaces, just maps and lists and charts pinned up with tacks. Everything was very clean and neat, but it didn't look like anyone lived there.

"I was never here much," he said lightly, as he saw her taking in the sterile atmosphere soberly. "It was just a place to crash between assignments."

"What are you going to do with it?" Jill asked.

"Well, the lease runs out in three months. The furniture is just what my mother left when she died. I'll take my clothes and whatever else I want to keep today and then let the Salvation Army come in and take the rest."

"You don't want any of it for our new place?" Jill said, putting her head on his shoulder, wondering how he could have lived this way for almost eight years. His had been a solitary, lonely existence, and it gave her new insight into the demons he faced when he fell in love with her on the job. How difficult it must have been for him to choose between the bureau, which represented the only stability he had known, and a sudden and unexpected love, which threatened that stability utterly.

"Well, soon-to-be Mrs. Barringer, I think I want a fresh start. Everything new. What do you say?"

"Fine with me, Mr. Barringer, just as long as I can bring my doll collection."

He feigned horror, tossing the empty suitcases he had brought with him onto the worn sofa.

"All those glassy eyes staring at me? Oh, all right. But keep them in a box or something." He went into the kitchen and ran the tap to get a glass of water. Jill followed and opened the refrigerator.

"Hmm. A bottle of club soda, a brown head of lettuce, a wedge of rock-hard cheese and a shriveled lemon quarter. What's for dinner?" Jill said.

He removed her hand from the door and shoved it closed. "I told you I was never here."

"But you must have spent some nights here when you were not working. Didn't you ever cook anything?"

"No."

"Never?"

"Never. I'd need directions to operate that oven." He took a sip of water and swallowed a pill.

"What's that?" Jill asked.

"Antibiotic."

"I thought you were done with those."

"Gilroy said to finish the bottle. I just have two of them left to take."

Jill still looked concerned. He set the glass on the counter and put his arm around her waist.

"Jill, it's just the prescription I took with me when I left the hospital. You've got to relax. I have recovered, I am well. We're getting married in three days. We're going to the Bahamas on our honeymoon. Joseph T. Craig is in the arms of the state of Massachusetts and very likely will stay there. Life is good."

Jill nodded. Most of the time she agreed with him, but once or twice a day she would have a moment when the terror came rushing back, when in her mind's eye she would see him clutch his chest and gasp and fall. Then she would have to shake off the feeling of dread and remind herself that Antony Barringer was healthy and that Joe Craig was in jail. And it was over.

"Come into the bedroom and help me decide what to take," he said, releasing her. She went with him and sat on the bed as he pulled sweaters and shirts out of drawers, tossing the garments into two piles—the keepers and the charity donations. From the top drawer he took a framed picture and tossed it into the keeper pile.

Jill got up and grabbed it.

"Who is this?" she asked.

"My mother."

Jill studied the photo, trying to see some resemblance between the young man she loved and the smiling woman in the high school graduation photo.

"You don't look like her," Jill finally said.

"No. Apparently I am the clone of her 'skipped to Down Under' husband, who took off with the proceeds of their meager joint accounts one fine day, leaving her with me, aged two, and little else." He tossed another shirt onto the discard pile.

"That must have been such a blow for her," Jill said quietly.

"Especially since every time she looked at me she must have seen my dear departed father. I even have his teeth," he said, tapping his slightly crooked eyetooth with his forefinger. He emptied a drawer and shoved it closed with his hip.

"Beautiful teeth," Jill said, and he grinned.

"Shucks, ma'am, you're makin' me blush." He repeated the procedure with the other drawers and the closet, rolling the discards up in the bedspread. Jill helped him take the clothes he wanted to keep and shove them into the suitcases in the living room. Finally he selected a pile of books from the apartment and put them in a cardboard box to carry out with them.

He looked around him briskly and said, "Okay, we're done. We can go. I'll call the charity—they said they would have a truck available next week."

"That's it? That's all you're going to take?"

He nodded.

"But…you must want something more. This was your home for several years."

"No. It was a place to sleep." He crossed the distance between them and said, "You're my home."

He picked up the suitcases, she took the box and turned out the light, and they left.

Jill and Tony were married in a short civil ceremony attended by Carrie, Michelle and Jill's father. Afterward they all went out to dinner and then the newlyweds caught an evening flight to Nassau. There they were shown into a gorgeous oceanfront suite with a balcony overlooking the beach, a glorious marble bathroom and a sitting room with a working fireplace, not likely to be used anytime soon but very decorative. A huge basket of fruit sat on the gilded coffee table and next to it a silver ice bucket that contained a bottle of champagne.

"Tony, this is fabulous," Jill said, looking around in awe. "Just one tiny question—how much are we paying for it?"

"Don't ask," Barringer said, opening the sliding balcony door and looking at the view. "Aah, feel that warm air. Quite a change from home.'' He turned to face her. "I figured we could afford it because I took that job at CranCo before we left.''

Jill gasped and then threw her arms around his neck. "Oh, Tony! Why didn't you tell me?''

"I wanted you to be surprised,'' he said, kissing her hair. "Are you surprised?''

"I am.''

"So you can finish school when we go home and get your master's degree.''

"Head of security. Pretty impressive.''

"Well, I'm an impressive guy. I think they saw that picture of me in the *Boston Herald,* you know the one with me out cold on the stretcher and said, 'That's the man for us!' ''

Jill shuddered. "Don't joke about it. I remember that picture. You looked dead.''

"A false image created in part by my ability to bleed copiously,'' he said, laughing. "Judy Campbell said that I was something of a curiosity among the nursing students.''

"I'll bet,'' Jill said dryly, stepping back from him.

He caught her hand. "Jealous?'' he teased.

"I swear every time I came to your hospital room to see you she was there.''

"I told you. I was exhibit A, the man who should be dead but is still talking.''

"Oh, don't be ridiculous. She was after you, even when she knew we were engaged.''

"Not very sporting of her, was it?'' he said mournfully, starting to unbutton her blouse.

"What are you doing?"

"Isn't it obvious?"

"The lifeguard at the pool is on duty until midnight, according to the sign downstairs. Don't you want to go for a swim?"

"No."

"Or have a late dinner? Room service runs until 2:00 a.m."

"No."

"Or listen to the band on the terrace? They play until the restaurant closes at eleven."

"No." He discarded her blouse and then pulled her chemise over her head.

"Don't need this, either," he said, tossing it on the sofa.

"Tony, we're in a five-star hotel in a beautiful place. Shouldn't we explore it?"

"I'd rather explore you."

"We can do this at home."

"I plan to do it at home. And here, and there, and everywhere." He unbuttoned the waistband of her skirt and let the garment slip to the floor.

"Don't you suppose you should rest for a while after the trip?" she asked faintly, as he knelt before her and pulled off her panties, his shiny new gold wedding band glinting in the soft light.

"Clothes are so unnecessary, don't you think?" he observed, ignoring her question as he rose and scooped her up in his arms.

"Tony, put me down! You shouldn't be carrying me, you know what Dr. Gilroy said..."

He set her on the bed and lay next to her as she added helplessly, ''I just don't want you to overdo it.''

He loomed over her, propped up on his elbows.

''Did anybody ever tell you that you talk too much?'' he asked.

Jill nodded. ''You.''

''I have the cure for the problem. Would you like me to share it with you?''

Jill smiled up at him. ''Yes.''

He kissed her, and silence fell.

*   *   *   *   *

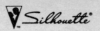

INTIMATE MOMENTS™

presents a riveting 12-book continuity series:

A Year of loving dangerously

Where passion rules and nothing is what it seems...

When dishonor threatens a top-secret agency, the brave
men and women of SPEAR are prepared to risk it all as they
put their lives—and their hearts—on the line.

Available December 2000:

STRANGERS WHEN WE MARRIED
by Carla Cassidy

Their courtship was whirlwind, their marriage passionate—and all
too brief. And now that his latest mission had sexy SPEAR agent
Seth Greene sharing a roof with his lovely wife once more, he knew
his greatest challenge lay ahead. For how could he convince his
long-lost bride that their love—their life together—was meant to be?

*Available only from Silhouette Intimate Moments
at your favorite retail outlet.*

Where love comes alive™

SPECIAL REPORT:
Peril and passion over Texas skies.

SAM HOUSTON INTERNATIONAL AIRPORT, Texas (AP)—In December 2000, authors **Merline Lovelace, Debra Cowan** and **Maggie Price** bring their pulse-pounding, heart-stopping three-in-one volume **SPECIAL REPORT** to Silhouette Intimate Moments. In this dramatic collection, the hijacking of a federal prisoner transport plane puts three couples' lives in danger—and their love to the test....

Available at your favorite retail outlet.

Where love comes alive™

Look Who's Celebrating Our 20th Anniversary:

"Happy 20th Anniversary, Silhouette! Your books have provided a lifetime of pleasure to me, and I couldn't have asked for better people with whom to work. I've treasured every minute of our association. Congratulations, and may you have twenty more."

—*New York Times* bestselling author
Linda Howard

"Life cannot promise 'happy-ever-after' endings, but Silhouette Books can and does. It is an honor and a privilege to be a part of the Silhouette family. Happy Anniversary, Silhouette Books, and a wish for many more years to come!"

—International bestselling author
Sharon Sala

"A toast to Silhouette! For twenty glorious years you have nourished hungry readers all over the world with warm, healthy, heart-y stories. I'm very proud to be part of such a remarkable tradition."

—International bestselling author
Kathleen Eagle

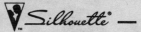

where love comes alive—online...

your romantic life

●—Romance 101——————
♥ Guides to romance, dating and flirting.

●—Dr. Romance ——————
♥ Get romance advice and tips from
our expert, Dr. Romance.

●—Recipes for Romance——
♥ How to plan romantic meals for you
and your sweetie.

●—Daily Love Dose——————
♥ Tips on how to keep the romance
alive every day.

●—Tales from the Heart——
♥ Discuss romantic dilemmas with other
members in our Tales from the Heart
message board.

SINTL1

#1 *New York Times* bestselling author

NORA ROBERTS

introduces the loyal and loving, tempestuous and
tantalizing Stanislaski family.

Coming in November 2000:

The Stanislaski Brothers
Mikhail and Alex

Their immigrant roots and warm, supportive home had
made Mikhail and Alex Stanislaski both strong and
passionate. And their charm makes them irresistible....

In February 2001, watch for
THE STANISLASKI SISTERS: Natasha and Rachel

And a brand-new Stanislaski story from Silhouette Special Edition,
CONSIDERING KATE

Available at your favorite retail outlet.

Where love comes alive™